ASSURED

NEW YORK TIMES & *USA TODAY* BESTSELLING AUTHOR

KAYLEE RYAN

Copyright © 2016 Kaylee Ryan
Second Edition

All Rights Reserved.
This book may not be reproduced in any manner whatsoever without the written permission of Kaylee Ryan, except for the use of brief quotations in articles and or reviews.

This book is a work of fiction. Names, characters, events, locations, businesses and plot are products of the author's imagination and meant to be used in a fictitious manner. Any resemblance to actual persons, living or dead, or actual events throughout the story are purely coincidental. The author acknowledges trademark owners and trademarked status of various products referenced in this work of fiction, which have been used without permission. The publication and use of these trademarks is not authorized, sponsored or associated by or with the trademark owners.
The following story contains sexual situations and strong language. It is intended for adult readers.

Cover Design: Perfect Pear Creative Covers
Cover Photography: Wander Aguiar
Cover Model: Jamie Walker
Editing: Hot Tree Editing
Formatting: Integrity Formatting

ASSURED

1. Confident.
2. Guaranteed; sure; certain; secure.
3. Boldly presumptuous.

CHAPTER 1

"YOU SURE ABOUT THIS, MAN?" I ask my best friend and bandmate, Kacen. I have to hold my fist up to my mouth to hide my smile. I know the question is ridiculous. All you have to do is see the way he looks at her.

Kacen doesn't even bother responding with words; instead, he gives me the look. You know, the one that says, "You're fucking crazy."

"There's still time to back out," Tristan chimes in. His grin is just as wide as mine.

"We got your back, just say the word," Gavin adds.

I lose my control as I throw my head back in laughter. Kacen just looks between the three of us, shaking his head. He knows that we all love Logan like a sister—the two of them are perfect for each other. It is, however, our job to ride him. That's what friends are for.

"Fuck off," he grumbles. "Nothing is going to stop me from marrying Logan today. If you jackasses want to try, there's the fucking door," he seethes.

"Whoa." I hold my hands up in surrender. "We're just giving you a hard time, Kace. You're too serious."

He focuses his angry eyes on me. "This *is* fucking serious!" he shouts. "What if she changes her mind, huh? What if she realizes that she doesn't want to be married to a rock star? What if she comes to her senses and figures out that she can do better?"

Seriously?

"For real?" Tristan asks. "Man, you and Logan are tight."

"What's got you all worked up?" Gavin questions.

Kacen plops down on the couch and rests his elbows on his knees. The three of us wait patiently for him to tell us what the hell is going through his head.

"I can't fucking breathe without her."

We've all been friends forever, so even with that one sentence, we get it. We get *him.* Kacen has always been different than the rest of us. He's not the guy who dips his stick into any available female; he's always been the responsible one, keeping the rest of us in line. That's actually how he met Logan—well, kind of. The guys and I had a hard time keeping our hands off our band's personal assistants over the years. Kacen finally got fed up and demanded a man be placed in the position. Logan was overqualified and hired sight unseen. Needless to say, it was a shock to all of us her first day; after all, we were expecting a male Logan, and we got the female version. The beautiful female version.

Turns out, she and her friend Stacy—who also happens to be a knockout—met Kace while on vacation, using their middle names. Anyway, long story short, they fell fast and hard and here we are, their wedding day.

"All right then, let's get this show on the road. We've got to get you to your ball and chain, and the boys and I"—I throw an arm over Gavin's and Tristan's shoulders—"have a bridal party to entertain." I waggle my eyebrows. Tristan and Gavin voice their agreement, while a slow smile crosses Kacen's face.

"Fucking finally. I'm going crazy waiting to make her mine."

"Get your ass down there. We've got some beautiful ladies to escort." Tristan winks, holding his fist out. Gavin and I follow suit.

"See you in a few," Kacen says as he rushes off to take his place.

"I always knew he would be the first," Tristan states.

"We got lucky. Logan's great. She makes him happy, and she's a hell of a cook," I chime in.

"Right?" Gavin agrees. "Let's hurry up so I can get out of this damn monkey suit," he says, pulling at his tie.

We make our way to where the bridesmaids and the bride are waiting for us. I discretely wipe my palms against the leg of my pants when I see her.

Stacy.

Stacy, who is the beautiful best friend of the bride, is my companion for the evening. Logan, of course, chose Stacy as her maid of honor, and the boys and I drew straws one night with Kacen. We were giving him shit about who he was going to choose as his best man—not that any one of us would be offended regardless, since we've all been friends for years. Anyway, Kace was getting frustrated and Logan blurted out that we should just draw straws, and now I am the lucky one who bears the title of best man. Don't get me wrong; I feel lucky and grateful for my man Kace, but the real luck comes with the fact that I'm paired with the lovely Stacy for the evening. I get to walk her down the aisle, we sit together at the wedding party table, and of course, after the newlyweds have their first dance, we as the wedding party must join them. I get to have my hands all over her, and I have an excuse!

Tonight is going to be fun.

Hence the reason my palms are sweaty. I've been trying to get my hands on this girl for weeks. From the minute I first saw her dancing in the club with Logan, she captured my attention. Since then, I've been pulling out all the stops and . . . nothing. Stacy gives as good as she gets; she flirts right back with me, but so far, I've been unsuccessful at seducing her.

I hope that changes tonight.

Our best friends are pledging to spend the rest of their lives together. It's all romantic and shit. Chicks love that. She's making me work for it, but that's fine. Once she finally gives in, she's going to wonder why she waited so long. I can guarantee, she won't be disappointed.

CHAPTER 2

Stacy

TODAY, MY BEST FRIEND MARRIES her best friend. Sounds crazy, right? If you were able to see the way they look at each other, though, you wouldn't think that way.

Logan and I are best friends. We talk about the men in our lives—well, currently her life, as I'm flying solo. We go shopping and to the salon together, and we are there for each other no matter what. Kacen, her soon-to-be husband, is also her best friend. Their friendship is on a more intimate level, one that only two souls that fuse together can share. I'm happy to say that I have been there from the beginning, and I could not be happier for the two of them. It's been a crazy ride so far, and I cannot wait to see what married life brings for them.

"Is it time yet?" Logan whines.

I can't help but laugh at her. She's *so* ready to walk down that aisle. She and Kacen have been in their own little world leading up to today.

"Actually, yes, it is. Are you sure you want to go through with this?"

"Seriously? Did you just ask me that?"

Her mouth hangs open as she stares at me.

"You know, Logan, we can sneak you out. We'll be gone before they realize what's happening," her cousin Lauren chimes in.

"I'll drive the getaway car," Cassidy says through her laughter.

It's obvious that we all know she's not going anywhere but toward the altar.

Toward Kacen.

Before she has a chance to put us in our place, there is a knock at the door. "Are you decent, Logan?" her mom asks, sticking her head in the door. "Your father is out here, and the guys are waiting on these beautiful ladies." She motions toward Lauren, Cassidy and me.

"YES!" she exclaims.

This causes me and the girls to burst out in laughter. "Stop, you're going to ruin my makeup," Cassidy snorts.

"All right, let me at my baby girl," Logan's father says, pushing into the room. "Ladies, you look beautiful as ever," he compliments, kissing his wife's cheek. Reaching out, he squeezes my shoulder quickly before his feet carry him to Logan. "You sure about this, Logan?" he asks.

"UGH!" Logan exclaims, causing the rest of us to fall back into a fit of laughter.

"What? You're always going to be my little girl. I need to make sure he makes you happy. Does he make you happy?" her dad asks. He almost sounds hopeful that she will say no. He loves Kacen, but as every father, they never want to let go of their little girls.

"You know I am, and he does. He's a part of me."

Leaning in, I watch with rapt attention as he kisses her forehead. "Yes, he does. That boy thinks the sun rises and sets with you."

"Boy?" Cassidy scoffs.

She's known Kacen and the rest of the Soul Serenade crew longer than the rest of us. I can only imagine the things she's seen. Although Kacen is the tamest of the four, I'm sure he has also had his fair share of moments.

"Hey! That's my husband you're talking about." Logan places her hands on her hips and mock-glares at Cassidy.

The excitement of what is about to happen shines in her eyes. She's as happy as I've ever seen her.

Logan's mom claps her hands. "Okay, let's do this. Ladies, the guys are at the end of the hall waiting on you. Let's get this one married." Her voice cracks and a sheen of tears clouds her eyes.

Cassidy and Lauren head for the door, and I head toward Logan, wrapping my arms around her. "I love you, bestie! I'm so fucking happy for you. It's time to marry your prince." Pulling away, I quickly swallow back the emotion clogging my throat and chase after Lauren and Cassidy.

At the end of the hall, I see them standing with the guys. I slow down and take my time getting to the group, drinking in the hotness that is Soul Serenade. Tristan and Gavin are talking with the girls, while Cole's eyes are locked on me. I flash him a flirty smile and his eyes darken. Since the day I first met Cole, he has been a relentless flirt. When Logan told me that we would be paired for the wedding, I knew I was going to have my hands full.

I know he wants me. I can see it in his eyes, the way they devour me any time the two of us are in the same room. Too bad I want more. A year ago, I would have jumped at the chance to spend a hot, lust-filled night with the long-haired, sexy-as-sin lead guitarist.

Not anymore.

Watching things unfold with Kacen and Logan has me realizing that I want the same thing. I don't want a casual hookup. I want the devoted, loving husband. I want the future my best friend is getting today. I'm insanely jealous and happy for her all at the same time.

Cole Hampton is not the type of guy to want more.

"Stacy," he murmurs as he reaches for my hand and pulls me to his side. His lips graze my cheek. "Looking lovely as ever," he coos.

Yes, coos. The man is laying it on thick. I'm going to have to work double time to resist him today. Cole in ripped jeans and a T-shirt is sexy, but Cole in a suit with his long hair pulled back into a bun is downright panty-dropping.

Must. Resist. Him.

"You clean up nice," I reply, tapping my hand against his solid chest. His grin is infectious.

"How's our girl?" Tristan asks me.

That's the thing about these guys—it's hard to push past their barriers but once you do, you're in. You're a part of them. They might be badass playboys, but every damn one of them has a heart of gold.

"She's ready. Kacen?"

All three of them break out in laughter. "He's something." Gavin chuckles. "We told him it wasn't too late to change his mind and I thought he was going to rip our heads off."

"We did the same thing to Logan. Those two." Lauren laughs, shaking her head.

"There she is," Cole exclaims.

Turning to look behind me, I see Logan in her gown, arm linked through her father's. She's breathtaking. Again, I fight back the emotions swarming me. It's going to be a long, emotional day. I can already tell.

Cole releases his hold on me and steps toward her. I watch as he leans down and kisses her cheek. I see his lips move but can't make out what he's saying. Whatever it is causes Logan's face to light up, her eyes welling with tears. Thank God for waterproof mascara.

Tristan and Gavin each take their turn greeting her. Just as Gavin pulls away, the wedding planner is there, clapping her hands together. "It's time, Ms. Andrews," she says, staring at the iPad in her hands.

"That's the last time you're going to hear that," Cole states with a grin. "Mrs. Warren," he winks at her. "Let's do this," he hooks his arm through mine and we take our place.

All the way down the aisle, his hand is gently caressing mine, which is wrapped around his elbow. Just as we reach the altar and are about to go to our places, I feel his hot breath against my ear. "I can't wait to hold this body next to mine on the dance floor." He nips at my lobe and gently releases me. I'm lucky I don't stumble and make a fool of myself.

This night is going to be interesting.

CHAPTER 3

SHE SMELLS FUCKING INCREDIBLE. LEANING in to whisper in her ear might not have been my smartest fucking move. Not only did I get to breathe her in, but I tasted her skin. The little hitch in her breath, the rise and fall of her chest—fuck me, I'm sporting wood, standing up here with my boy on the biggest day of his life. *Puppies. Kittens. Grandma Iris.*

Finally, my cock starts to deflate. I focus my attention to watch the rest of our crew walking down the aisle.

Logan appears, and my man, Kacen, sways on his feet. "Holy fuck," he whispers. I bring my fist to my mouth and pretend to cough to smother my laugh. It's always been like this for him. I knew the first time I saw him look at her, even though he was confused at what she was doing in his house, that she was different for him. I don't understand it, but I get it. Kacen has always wanted what Logan is giving him—to settle down and have a few kids. I like kids, but I've never thought much about having my own.

Hell, I'm living the dream right now. Maybe somewhere down the road.

Kacen shuffles his weight from foot to foot, and I realize that he's losing his shit. Any time he's in the same room with her, he has to be as close as possible. If I know my boy, he's thinking about running down the aisle and throwing his bride over his shoulder, moving the ceremony along.

I lean in and whisper in his ear, "Chill, Kace She's all yours. Just take a deep breath."

I hear him suck in air and slowly exhale just as Logan steps in front of him. "You're so fucking beautiful," he says, not bothering to lower his voice. The guys laugh and the girls "Awww" over his declaration. Logan grins widely as tears shimmer in her eyes.

I have to hand it to him—he picked a good one. She's gorgeous, down-to-earth, and she can cook. I'm sure that's not what made him fall in love with her, but they're all good qualities if you ask me.

The ceremony is quick and painless. Of course, I spent most of my time watching Stacy. She caught me a few times, but I just gave her a wink and kept staring. She knows I'm interested; now I just have to get her on board. But this girl is not making it easy on me. It's kind of refreshing since I don't usually have to work for it. She's making it . . . fun.

As soon as Logan says I do, Kacen pulls her into a kiss. Lifting her off her fit and crushing her to him. "Fucking finally. Logan Warren," his voice echoes throughout the room.

The room erupts in cheers, but by the looks of the happy couple you would never know it. Kacen has Logan pulled close with his forehead resting against hers. They are both wearing blinding smiles.

The crowd starts to dwindle as they head to the reception. The wedding party is still standing at the front of the room with the newlyweds. It's not at all how we practiced in the wedding rehearsal last night. This is so much better.

The reception is in full swing and, just like I suspected, me being paired with Stacy is in my favor. I need to remember to thank Logan and Kacen. Currently, we are sitting at a long table, the six of us paired off and waiting for Mr. and Mrs. Kacen Warren to make their appearance. If I know my boy, he's celebrating the fact that Logan is finally his, name changed and all that shit he was spouting off about earlier.

I sit back in my seat and rest my arm on the back of Stacy's chair. She's talking to Lauren, who is sitting beside her, and she doesn't miss a beat in her conversation. Her words don't falter; she doesn't move an inch or even turn to look at me. I need to step up my game.

I lean toward her and begin to run my finger over her bare shoulder. Goose bumps break out against her skin.

Jackpot!

I trace her soft skin and sip my beer, acting as though it's the most normal thing in the world. In my mind it is. Only I imagine tracing said skin with my tongue.

Tristan, who is on the other side of Lauren, asks her a question, which steals her attention from Stacy. Feeling brave, I lean in close and whisper, "Your skin is so soft."

Again the goose bumps, only this time I can see a slight tremor in her shoulders.

Perfect.

"It's not going to work, Hampton." She laughs. It's not her normal, "I'm cutting up with you, that's funny" laugh. No, this laugh is . . . nervous. I'm making her nervous. Score, Hampton!

"What's not going to work?" I feign innocence.

She glances over at me and smiles softly, shaking her head. I'm bringing my A game tonight. I want this girl, have for months. She's not going to know what hit her.

"Ladies and gentlemen, may I have your attention." The wedding planner's voice rings through the reception hall. "I would like to introduce you to Mr. and Mrs. Kacen Warren." The room breaks out in applause. "The bride and groom will take their first dance as man and wife. The wedding party will then join for the second dance," she announces.

In any other situation, I would be irritated with this shit. But this is for my boy and Logan. Not to mention I get to hold Stacy's tight little body next to mine, just like I told her I would.

Fucking finally!

Stacy reaches for her wine glass and slowly drains it. Liquid courage, I'm sure. I know my words from earlier are bouncing around in that little head of hers.

Kacen and Logan's dance is over and guests break out in a chant of "Kiss, kiss, kiss." Not having to be told, but willing to go with it, Kacen dips Logan over his arm and lays a smoking-hot kiss on her.

The wedding planner motions for us, and I stand and reach for Stacy's hand. "That's our cue, sweets." I watch as she stares longingly at her empty champagne glass before relenting and placing her hand in mine. Gripping it tightly, I place my other hand on the small of her back. I'm taking every excuse I can think of to touch her.

As Steven Tyler's voice comes through the sound system, I pull Stacy in to my chest and clasp my hands on the small of her back. I feel her try to take a step back, but I just tighten my hold on her. *Not happening, sweetheart.*

"Is it as good as you thought it would be?" I ask her.

She raises her head in confusion, those green eyes taking me in. "What?" she asks hesitantly.

Leaning close—one, so I can breathe her in and two, because I know the effect it has on her—I whisper in her ear. "This. Being in my arms."

A smile lights up her face as she throws her head back in laughter. "You're too much."

You have no idea, baby.

CHAPTER 4

Stacy

BREATHE IN. BREATHE OUT.

I have to keep reminding myself. Cole is the definition of sexy. He's tall, lean—and that hair. I hate to admit that I'm envious of his brown locks. My hands are resting on his shoulder, itching to pull that elastic band holding his bun at the top of his head, letting it fall around his shoulders. I'm not ashamed to admit that I've spent many nights fantasizing about running my fingers through his hair, holding on tight when he . . . Focus, Stacy.

I laugh nervously at his comment and focus on the other couples around us. Logan and Kacen are blissfully happy, doing their thing, and from the looks of it, Lauren and Tristan are as well. Gavin and Cassidy are in deep conversation. None of them are aware of my inner turmoil.

Soft yet firm lips press against my neck, capturing my attention.

Cole.

Sexy.

Relentless.

Trouble.

"You are so fucking sexy," he growls. Yes, he growls in my ear, his lips trailing up my neck. He's pulling out all the stops tonight. This is new for us.

Shit.

I need a drink.

"Cole. . . ."

"Stacy," his deep voice rumbles in my ear.

"What are you doing?" I ask the question, but my sex-starved brain tilts my head to the side, giving him access. Those lips, though.

"Trying to seduce you." At least he's honest. "Is it working?"

Is it? Fuck me, but it could. It would be so easy to fall into a night of passion with him. Let him have his wicked way with me.

Yes, please!

"Cole, you know this can't happen. We can't happen," I say instead.

"Oh, sweetheart, it can," he replies, nipping at my earlobe.

Holy fucking shit! He's lethal to my libido. Thankfully, the song changes, allowing me to gather my wits and pull away from him. "Thank you for the dance," I say, before I turn and hightail it back to the table. I know that I'll still have to sit next to him, but at least our bodies won't be pressed together. His lips won't be against my heated skin.

Distance. That's what I need.

On my way back to the table, I grab a fresh glass of champagne from a passing waiter. It's gone by the time I make it to my seat. Luckily, my bestie married a rich-as-hell rock star who hired more servers than needed. As soon as my ass hits the seat, a waitress appears beside me, offering another glass. This time, I take two.

My second glass is gone by the time Cole takes his seat beside me. He throws his arm over the back of my chair and resumes his previous torture of running his finger across my shoulders. I was able to ignore it before our dance, but now? Not only does a chill break out across my skin, but I feel it . . . everywhere. Not willing to look at him, I tip back my third glass of champagne in less than five minutes. I know I need to slow down, but I welcome the calm it brings me.

Cole has me on edge.

Tristan leans over in front of Lauren to ask Cole a question. This has Cole doing the same thing. He leans in to me, his chest against the bare skin of my arm. His arm, which used to be on the back of the chair, now rests on my shoulders, his scent once again surrounding me. Lauren is chatting with the guys, not a care in the world that Tristan is all up in her personal space. Normally, that would be me. That *should* be me, but Cole is . . . intense. He's not a guy who is used to being told no. So really, I only have myself to blame.

He wants the chase.

Before I downed those three glasses of bubbly, I was sure that I didn't want to be caught. Now . . . now I want another glass of champagne. Miraculously, the waitress once again appears and I grab two more glasses, making a mental note to tell Kacen he did good with the wait staff.

"Might want to slow down, babe," Cole says, his hot breath against my cheek.

Nope. Definitely need more. "It's a celebration," I defend my sudden need for liquid courage.

I feel his eyes on me as I gulp yet another glass. He doesn't try to stop me, but he does scoot a little closer.

I can't help but thinking that I'm fucked. And soon will be literally, as I reach for yet another glass. The three of them continue to chat—about what, I'm not sure; I can't pay attention with the heat from his body seeping into mine. His hand resting on my bare shoulder.

Movement draws my attention, and I see it's Lauren and Tristan getting up from the table. I see that Gavin and Cassidy are following them. "Where are they going?" Even I can hear the panic in my voice. It's not like Cole's going to throw me on the table and have his wicked way with me right here in the middle of the reception hall or anything.

Great! Now that's what I'm thinking about.

Cole is still leaning in to me, and he brings his lips close to mine. "Dancing. You want to join them?"

"N-no."

"It's a slow one. I could pull you close, align that tight little body with mine." He kisses the corner of my mouth before he trails his lips across my jaw, working his way to my ear. "This is good too. I can sit here and get you ready for me. Make you want me so bad that you're the one dragging me away from the eyes of all these people."

It takes a minute for my brain to catch up to the fact that we are indeed sitting at the front of the room, giving everyone a show. "Fine, let's dance." At least on the dance floor, we can blend in with everyone else. Sitting here is too much like we're together, and we are most definitely not.

Cole grins. "After you, sweets." He stands, offering me his hand.

Trouble. I'm in big trouble.

CHAPTER 5

As I lead Stacy out on the dance floor for the second time, I have to reach out and steady her. I'm not surprised after the amount of champagne she just consumed in such a short span of time. Hopefully, we can work some of it out of her system on the dance floor.

We reach the crowd of dancers and I pull her to me; this time, she doesn't resist. She clasps her hands behind my neck and lets me hold her close. I'm hard as steel, and when she whips her head up to look at me, those green eyes wide, I know she can feel me. Hands on her hips, I pull her as close as I can get her. Bending down, I whisper in her ear, "That's all you, Stacy. I ache to be inside you."

She whimpers, and I have to fight my grin. *Fucking finally!* Leaning in, she rests her head against my chest. Looking down, I watch as her eyes flutter closed, see the rapid rise and fall of her chest. She wants this just as badly as I do.

As the song changes from slow to sensual, I rock my hips against her, and it's like that move alone caused some type of switch to go off. She lifts her head, flashes me a flirty grin, and mimics my movements. My cock takes notice to the point that it's painful. Not willing to lose an opportunity to touch her, I take the lead as our bodies grind to the beat.

Push and pull.

Pain and pleasure.

I want her.

Again, the music changes, and I send a mental high five to the DJ. Stacy's big eyes find mine. "I want to run my fingers through it."

It takes me a minute to figure out what she's talking about. My hair.

"What else do you want to do to me?"

She flashes me a sexy smile and opens her mouth, but the words never come because Logan and Kacen appear beside us. "Stacy, you mind running up to the room with me? I want to change these shoes, and if my husband goes with me, we might not make it back." She giggles as Kacen kisses her neck.

She immediately removes her hands from around my neck and steps back. Reluctantly, I let her go.

Logan reaches for her hand, pulling her toward the exit. "We'll be right back!" she yells over her shoulder.

"You're drooling." I elbow Kacen to get his attention. Luckily, his eyes followed his new bride so he didn't notice that I ogled the lovely Stacy until they were out of sight.

Turning to look at me, he's wearing a goofy-ass grin. "She's mine."

Such a simple statement, yet it means so much more. I can't help but get sentimental. "I'm happy for you, man. You deserve this."

"Thanks, C." He turns back to stare at the door where the girls disappeared.

"Let's get you a beer." I clamp a hand down on his shoulder and turn us toward the bar.

"I'm good," he says, taking a stool.

I raise my eyebrows in silent question.

"Dude, she's my fucking wife. As soon as I convince her that we've spent enough time down here,"—he points to the dance floor—"I'm taking her upstairs and ravishing her. It will be a cold day in hell that I'm not sober enough to remember sliding into her as my wife for the first time."

I nod, because really, what else can I say? He has a valid point, and even though I've never been the settling-down type, I can see where he's coming from. There are just some moments that you want a vivid memory of that will last you a lifetime.

"So, you and Stacy looked cozy."

I nod again, before bringing the cold beer the bartender just handed me to my lips. "She's hot as hell."

"That she is, but she is also my wife's best friend. Your friend's best friend."

Is he warning me to stay away from her? We've had conversations like this before, since the boys and I have run off a few of the band's personal assistants over the years. It's not our fault they thought they could "change" us.

"And?"

"And don't fuck with her. Logan is my wife. She's permanent. Stacy is her best friend—also permanent. I don't want things to be awkward. We all spend a hell of a lot of time together, and we don't need that shit. None of us."

Fuck me.

"They're back. Think about it, man." He doesn't say another word until Logan is within reach. "There's my wife."

She giggles. "Miss me?"

He doesn't answer her, instead pulling her to him before kissing the fuck out of her. Turning away from them, I see Stacy reaching for another glass of champagne from a passing waiter.

Setting my half-empty beer bottle on the bar, I snake my arm out and pull her close. "You good?"

Bringing the glass to her lips, she tips it back and drains it. With a coy smile, she says, "Yep."

My eyes follow her lips as her tongue slips out and licks a tiny of drop of champagne.

"Let's do this," Logan's voice breaks through my haze of lust as she pulls Stacy onto the dance floor.

I watch her. Every fucking step she takes, my eyes are glued to her. It's obvious from the slow, easy sway of her body to the beat of the music that she's more than a little tipsy. I'm glad she's out there with Logan; dancing her ass off will help sober her up.

I'm going to need her sober.

CHAPTER 6

Stacy

I'M DRUNK. NOT "I WON'T remember tomorrow" drunk, but enough to let my inhibitions go. Enough that I'm actually considering taking Cole up on his offer for some sexy time. He's hot as hell and has been coming on strong all night. I'm drunk enough to consider it, to consider *him,* but not enough to go through with it.

At least not yet.

I close my eyes and let the music guide me, blocking out the fact that the sexy guitar player is more than likely watching me. Throwing my arms in the air, I sway my hips and use the image of those big brown eyes on me as my motivation to drive him crazy. After all, he's been relentless from day one. I usually just flirt back or blow him off. Not tonight. Tonight, I'm stepping up my game. I'm going to torture him like he has me for months now. He knows it won't work for us. He knows that us giving in to this . . . chemistry will cause nothing but awkwardness between our group, and no way am I going to let that happen.

"I need a drink!" Logan yells over the music.

I nod my agreement—a drink is exactly what I need. Logan grabs my hand, guides us to the bar, and orders us a shot of tequila each.

Perfect.

"Bottoms up, bestie." Logan pushes both shots toward me as she uncaps a bottle of water.

Wait, what? "Logan?" Her eyes sparkle and I know. She's pregnant. "Does Kacen know?"

Her smile is blinding as she nods. Holy shit! I quickly down both shots, one right after the other, and slam the glasses down on the bar. I turn toward Logan and throw my arms around her. A baby!

"I can't believe this! Were you trying?" I ask after stepping back, allowing her room to breathe.

Logan throws her head back and laughs. "Not at all, but we're happy about it. Kacen is ecstatic. I actually just told him earlier tonight. My wedding gift." She beams with happiness.

"Holy shit!" I let my earlier thoughts fall from my lips. "You're going to be a mom." Logan nods as I reach out and rest my hand against her belly.

"What are you ladies doing over here?" Kacen asks as he slips in behind her, wrapping his arms around her waist.

"Oh, you know, just girl talk."

"Is that so?" Kacen nuzzles her ear.

"Congratulations," I tell them both. Kacen looks up and smiles.

"Thanks, Stace. We're happy about it."

"What am I missing?" Cole asks from beside me, his arm suddenly wrapped around me, hand resting on my hip. How did I miss that?

"I didn't know if she was ready to tell people. I just found out myself," Kacen explains.

"Found out about what?" Cole asks again.

"My wife and I are having a baby."

The newlyweds are wearing matching grins as they wait for Cole's reaction. I admit that I'm a little curious as to what he will say as well. I don't have to wait long.

"No shit?" he asks. A slow smile tips his lips before he steps forward and wraps them both in a hug. "Congratulations, guys. You *are* naming him after me, right?"

Not at all the reaction I suspected. For some reason, I didn't see the "playboy" Cole Hampton being happy for his friend and fellow bandmate. I expected him to spout some bullshit about the upcoming tour or something to that effect.

Feeling a little off balance from those last two shots, I step back to lean against the bar and stumble. Cole is there, sliding his arm around my waist and pulling me toward him. "I got you, sweets," he murmurs, his hot breath hitting my ear.

His scent surrounds me. "You smell good."

I can feel the vibration of his chest as he pulls me against him. "And you're cute when you're drunk."

"Not drunk," I mumble into his chest. Not that he can hear me.

"I think those last two shots did her in," Logan says.

"I got her. You guys go ahead," Cole tells them as he wraps me tighter in his arms.

I attempt to pull away from him, but his hold is firm. He's warm and comfortable and smells good enough to eat. I don't put up much of a fight. Definitely the alcohol.

The three of them are talking—about me, I'm sure, but I just can't seem to make myself care what they're saying. I'm going to lean here against his solid chest. Let him wrap those strong arms around me, and relish the feeling. Drunk or not, this is something I've thought about since I first met him, but would never let my guard down long enough to allow happen.

Tonight, I'm breaking all the damn rules. I'm going to soak up this feeling for just a few more minutes. At least I can blame it on the alcohol.

CHAPTER 7

"TAKE YOUR WIFE UPSTAIRS AND ravish her. I got this one." I give Stacy's hip a gentle squeeze.

"Cole," Kacen practically growls my name.

"Dial in the inner caveman there, Daddy. I told you I got her. I'll make sure that she gets to her room safe and sound." I smirk at him because he's making this too damn easy.

I want to fuck her. This is common knowledge—I don't hide my feelings from anyone, especially her. However, I want her to remember it. I want to ruin her for other men. She has me wound tight, and yeah . . . she's gonna need to be sober for what I have planned.

"Dammit!" Kacen exclaims.

Logan darts her eyes back and forth between the three of us. She doesn't seem to be as concerned for her friend as she is for her husband; she's more worried about Kacen and the words that are flying from his mouth.

"I fucking told you, C."

"You're right, you did, and I heard every fucking word."

"Babe, he'll take care of her," Logan tries to calm him.

Logan has always been that way. No matter the rumors she's heard about us, she's always taken our side. Not just because of Kacen, but because that's the kind of person she is. She knows I would never take advantage of a drunken girl, ever. I may like to play around, but I'm not an asshole.

"Listen to your wife, Kace. I give you my word." Tonight. All bets are off when she sobers up.

He stares at me for what seems like hours, even though it's only a few seconds at the most. He must find what he's looking for, because he nods and laces his fingers through Logan's. Without further argument, he guides them out of the ballroom.

I glance down at Stacy; her eyes are closed, and she looks so damn peaceful.

Beautiful.

"All right, you. Let's get you up to your room. Can you walk?" I have no idea if she's even awake. I don't get a reply, so without losing my grip on her, so she doesn't fall, I very carefully pull away from her and lift her into my arms. I scan the room and see that Tristan is still on the dance floor, all wrapped up in Logan's cousin. I think her name is Lauren. My eyes roaming around the room, I find Gavin sitting next to Cassidy. They both seem to be lost in thought as they watch the remaining guests. My boys are good; time to get this damsel in distress up to her room.

I manage to hit the Call button for the elevator without dropping her. When the car finally arrives, I again work to hit her floor—well, our floor. Kace rented the whole damn thing, along with the honeymoon suite. I rest my back against the wall of the elevator and watch as the numbers climbs. Looking down to the beautiful mess in my arms, I can't help but smile. This is not how I wanted this night to end, but I have to admit that getting to see her like this, so relaxed, is a nice change from what I usually get. She always seems on her guard around me. I tell myself it's because she feels this sexual energy between us, but really I can't be sure that's what it is. A man can hope.

Reaching our floor, I realize I don't have a key to her room. Shit! I stand there in the middle of the hall, not sure of my next move. I guess I'm going to have to set her down so I can call downstairs. From the looks of this slinky dress she has on, there is nowhere to hide a key card. I spot a bench just down the hall and head that way. I try to carefully place her on it, but her grip around my neck is tight.

"This isn't my room."

Ah, she's awake. "No, sweets, I need you to let go so I can call down to get a key."

"I got my key." She releases her hold around my neck and begins to inch up her dress. I place my hand over hers to stop her progress. I'm not getting under there, so I don't need to see that shit.

"Let me get it."

"Stacy, babe, where do you think you're going to get your key?" I'm at a loss for words right now.

She throws my hand off hers, wiggles her ass against the bench, and works her dress up over her thighs.

Fuck me.

I watch with rapt attention as a white garter comes into view. I'm waiting for her to reveal more, knowing it's a bad idea, but unable to look away if my life depended upon it.

I watch as her fingers slip into the garter and slide out with a white key card. Fuck, that's hot. She holds it in the air like a prize and gives me a goofy grin. "Ta-da!"

Her drunken excitement is infectious, but then again, maybe it's just her. I grab the card from her hands and swiftly sweep her back into my arms. Her hands instantly clasp around my neck. "A girl could get used to this," she whispers.

My first thought is "Don't." My next is that a girl like her deserves to get used to being treated right. As soon as the thought comes, I shake it off. This wedding has got me waxing all kinds of fucked-up poetic in my brain. I shouldn't be thinking that shit. I should be thinking about what it's going to be like when I finally get to bury myself deep inside her. Fuck, no, that's not good either. Now I'm hard as fuck with no relief in sight.

Reaching her room, I pull off some ninja skills to unlock her door, getting us both inside without incident. The door closes behind us, and I toss the key onto the dresser as I make my way to the king-sized bed, which takes up most of the room.

I lay her on the bed and reach back to untangle her hands from around my neck, but she has other plans. Before I realize it, her lips are on mine.

Hot.

Wet.

Fuck!

It may be an asshole move, but I'm not letting the opportunity to taste her pass me by. Not a fucking chance.

Leaning in to her, I deepen the kiss. Her lips part for me, as do her legs. She slowly slides further onto the bed and I follow after her, drinking her in. I'm lost in the moment, fighting for control. When her hips lift and rub against my cock, nestled between her legs, I know I have to rein myself in. Just my fucking luck that she's drunk off her ass.

I slow the kiss and pepper a few against her jaw before lifting my weight off her. Unfortunately, this pushes my cock against her hot center.

"Cole." She moans my name like a fucking porn star, reaching up to my neck. Before I know what she's doing, she's removing the band that holds my hair up and it falls over my shoulders. "I've wanted to do this all night," she says as she begins running her fingers through my hair.

My hips have a mind of their own as they rock into her, causing yet another moan. Fuck, I need to stop before I do something she'll regret in the morning. I would feel guilty, but something tells me I would never regret being inside her. She's just. . . . Yeah, no regrets on my end.

When I try to pull my hips from her heat, she wraps her legs around me. "Don't go."

Fuck! She's killing my restraint.

"We have to stop. You'll regret it if you don't."

"I won't," she slurs.

Yes, you will. Relaxing back in to her, I place my lips next to her ear. "I want you sober when you allow me inside you. You're going to need all your energy." I nip her ear and quickly climb off the bed, off her.

Running my fingers through my hair, I realize I don't know where the tie went. Stacy clears her throat. I close my eyes tight, willing myself to look at her and not devour her.

God, give me strength.

Slowly, I open my eyes and she's sitting up on her elbows, hair a mess, eyes glassy, lips swollen by mine. She sits up all the way and reaches out to me. In her hand is my tie.

"Thank you." I reach for it, but she closes her hand tight.

"Don't go." Her eyes are locked on mine, trying to tell me . . . something. It's a lost effort, though, because my cock is thinking for me right now. He's telling me to take what she's offering.

"I have to, sweets." My voice is gruff. "If I stay, you'll hate me tomorrow and regardless of what you or anyone else thinks, I'm not okay with that outcome." Bending down, I kiss her cheek. Her hand falls open and I grab the tie. Once I have my hair pulled back in a knot, I chance another look at her. "I want you, Stacy. I've wanted you for months now, but not like this. Our time is coming, babe, and when it gets here, we're going to set the fucking house on fire."

Needing to get out of there and away from temptation, I turn and walk out of her room.

CHAPTER 8

Stacy

THE SUN BLAZING THROUGH THE windows has me throwing my arm over my eyes. My head is pounding and my mouth tastes like ass—well, what I would suspect ass tastes like. My tired eyes blink away the fog and slowly open. I survey my surroundings and come to the conclusion that I am indeed in my hotel room. Scenes from last night flash through my mind, but they're hazy at best.

What the hell happened?

Throwing the covers off, I see that I'm still in my dress from the wedding. *Well, at least there's that. Good to know I more than likely slept alone last night.* Slowly, I pull myself to a sitting position. UGH! I need the bathroom, a bottle of water and some headache medicine, stat.

I wince at a sudden knock on the door. Glancing at the clock on the bedside table, I see that it's still early. Too early for the newlyweds to be out and about. Gingerly, I lower my feet to the floor and pad my way to the door. I don't bother asking who it is; at this point, whoever it is will be shot down. I'm in need of some hygiene attention, right after that headache medicine.

I pull open the door and cringe when I see Cole standing there.

"Well, that's not a greeting I'm used to getting." He smirks.

Shit. I look like I've been rode hard and put up wet. Well, at least once he gets a good look he'll stop with this "you will be under me" bullshit. He'll know exactly what he would be waking up to. Then again, I can't see Cole as the "let's spend the night and cuddle" type. From what I've heard, he's more of a "let me rock your word and then roll out" kind of guy.

"What the hell are you doing up so early?"

Cole steps in, crowding my space, inviting himself into my room.

"Come on in," I say dryly.

"I helped you back to your room last night. I knew you would be feeling like . . . well, how you look this morning, so I brought supplies." He holds up a tray with two coffees and a bag from the bakery downstairs.

I take the offered bag and peek inside. Fresh doughnuts. Yum!

"Oh, and this." He reaches into his front pocket and pulls out a small bottle of Advil.

"Gimme." I hold out my hand for the bottle. Cole Hampton is a lifesaver. Never thought I would be saying that.

He chuckles and hands it over. "Safe to say I made a good decision?"

"Yes. Thank you." I swallow three pills and chase them with coffee, burning my tongue in the process. "Thanks for stopping by, but I have to pee, shower and scrub my mouth for at least an hour. Make sure the door is locked when you leave," I call over my shoulder. It's a bitchy thing to do, but he smells incredible. His tight jeans and that messy bun have him looking all sexy, and I look and feel like death warmed over. The self-conscious part of me kicked in, and in turn bitch mode broke loose. I feel a little guilty, but Cole is a big boy—he can handle it.

To be honest, I'm a little disappointed that this cat and mouse game we've been playing has come to an end. He's seen me at my worst; no way he's going to continue the pursuit. It's better off that way, but damn if it's not fun going back and forth with him. Yesterday was the exception. Usually I'm not so . . . close, and no hands are involved. Dancing so close to him just about had me breaking my resolve.

Stripping down, I start the shower; I need the water nice and hot to break away this funk. I spend several minutes brushing my teeth before submerging myself into the hot spray, moaning at the feel of it against my sore muscles. I must have slept in the same position all night.

I take my time, enjoying the warm water against my skin. Whoever invented the shower was a pure genius.

Stepping out, I wrap my hair in a towel and wrap another around my body.

"That's a good look for you."

I scream at the sound of Cole's voice. Shit! "I thought you were leaving?" I tighten my hold on the towel.

"Why would I do that? I'm glad I didn't, seeing as how I get to see . . . this." He points from my head to my toes. "This is definitely not something I would want to miss out on."

Well, I guess seeing me look like death didn't deter him. "There's nothing to see here."

"Oh, sweets, I beg to differ."

Gah! This man is so damn frustrating. "You can go now. I survived the shower."

"Nope, you go on ahead and do your thing. Pretend I'm not even here." He smirks.

Right. Cole Hampton being within a hundred-mile radius is hard to ignore. Sitting in my hotel room, with me in nothing but a cotton towel? Impossible.

"What are you doing here again?"

"Besides bringing you the hangover cure, I'm your ride home, remember?"

Shit! Now I do. I rode over in the limo with Logan, so Kacen arranged for Cole to take me home since he and Logan would be off on their honeymoon.

"Let me get dressed."

"Don't do that on my account. I've got nothing but time."

Still holding the towel, just in case, I quickly grab my clothes and rush into the bathroom, this time locking the door. Not that I think he'll come busting in or anything. I was naked and he didn't try, so my guess is that I'm good, but it's not worth the chance. But Cole is deliciously tempting—all six-foot-four of him. There needs to be safeguards in place.

CHAPTER 9

RESTRAINT. I NEED A FUCKING medal or something. I could hear her moan when she stepped into the shower. It took more willpower than I knew I possessed to not bust into the bathroom and take her. I'm out of my element here. I don't want to treat her like a good time and then toss her—I know she's better than that. Besides, Kacen's warning keeps ringing in my damn ears. Fuck! He needs to get out of my head.

I'm sitting here in her hotel room with her while she's naked. *Naked!* I never hesitate, but my boy is all up in my head telling me that she's permanent. That word—permanent. That's not a word I would associate with women; never has a woman other than my mom or my sister been in that category. Regardless, it doesn't change the fact that I want her, ache to be inside her, and I have for months. I just need to not do it today. That way, I can be honest when I tell Kace I didn't fuck her after the wedding. But after today, after we leave this hotel? All bets are off.

I shift in my seat and adjust my cock, which is angry as hell that we're passing on what he thinks could have been ours today. I'm just as disappointed as he is.

"It will just take me a minute to get packed up." Stacy's voice pulls me from my thoughts. Thoughts of her and my cock.

I run my fingers over my eyes. I'm a mess today. I'm sure it's because I've tasted her, and from her surprise at seeing me at her door this morning, she doesn't remember any of it. Just like I knew she wouldn't.

"I got nothing but time, sweets."

She busies herself running around the room like a little hurricane, gathering everything and shoving it into her suitcase.

"Okay, I think that's everything." She lugs the suitcase off the bed and wheels it toward me.

I reach out and take the handle from her. "Sounds good. You hungry?"

"Um . . . yes."

Her answer is cautious, as if she's trying to figure out why I would ask. "Good, I'm starving. That damn doughnut didn't even touch my appetite." I don't wait for her to respond, instead wheeling her suitcase to the door, which I hold open for her. She hesitates before releasing a heavy sigh and walking out the door.

As we stand and wait for the elevator, thoughts of last night flash through my mind. "So, you don't really have to check out, just turn in your key. Kacen and Logan took care of it." I try to control the conversation to keep my mind off the fact that I just had the woman I've been lusting after in a hotel room and left voluntarily without even trying to get with her.

An amused chuckle falls from my lips.

"What's so funny?"

"I had you alone, naked, and here we are leaving said location." Honesty is always the best policy in my eyes. That's something no one will have to worry about from me.

"I'm just as surprised as you are."

Wait, what? "Meaning?" I ask. *Is she saying what I think she is?*

"Just that you've been a relentless flirt for months now. I'm surprised that when it's just the two of us, you clam up." She smirks.

"Clam up? Woman, I'm trying to be respectful." *Does she seriously think that I "clammed up"?*

"I'm just saying. It doesn't make sense to me. I guess you're all talk and no action."

What. The. Fuck?

Reaching over, I hit the Stop button on the elevator.

"What the hell are you doing?" she shrieks.

I abandon her suitcase and stalk toward her. She tries to back up, but she's already leaning against the wall, palms flat. I place mine on either side of her head, caging her in. "Trust me, sweets. I still want you. I want to slide into that tight little body and get lost in you. I'm being respectful. Kacen made me promise not to make a move last night, because you were wasted. I promised my best friend that you would be safe from me. Not to mention I want you to remember the moment that it happens. Remember every detail of when I slide inside you. As soon as this day is over, all bets are off. He knows I want you. *You* know I want you." I lean in a little closer and push my hard length against her belly. "Does this feel 'clammed up' to you, Stacy?"

Her breath hitches as her chest rapidly rises and falls. I watch as her tongue slips out and runs across her lips. She's not unaffected by me like she wants me to think.

"Yeah, you and me? We're going to happen. It's not a matter of 'if,' sweets. It's 'when.'"

"Cocky," she breathes.

"Assured," I fire back.

If she only knew the thoughts that I've had about her, about us. *Clammed up. Pfft.*

"They're going to wonder what happened." She looks over at the control panel.

Slowly, I pull away from her, reaching over and hitting the button that will resume our descent to the first floor. I step as far away as I can get, but I never take my eyes off her. She's trying to get herself under control; I see it with every deep breath that she takes.

A gold fucking Olympic medal for the restraint it's taking to not have my way with her. Kacen is just going to have to deal.

CHAPTER 10

I REMEMBER LOGAN REFERRING TO Kacen as Hurricane Kacen. I think I now understand what she meant. Cole is . . . intense and sexy and cocky as hell. That's not usually an attribute that I'm into, but it works for him.

"This okay?" he asks as he pulls into the lot of a small mom-and-pop diner.

It's perfect. I'd rather be here than a big fancy restaurant chain any day.

"Yeah," I say instead—I don't need his ego inflating any further. I climb out of the truck and meet him in the front. He opens the door for me, not that I'm surprised; just because he likes variety in his bed doesn't mean he's an asshole. All four of the Soul Serenade members are great guys.

His hand rests on the small of my back as he guides us to a booth in the back of the diner. It's a sweet gesture, and it's when he's like this that I'm in the most danger of giving into him. In this moment, he's not Cole Hampton, lead guitarist for Soul Serenade. Here, he's just Cole.

Before we are even settled, an older lady with silver hair appears beside us. "Cole, good to see you. Where is the rest of the clan?" she asks, laying menus in front of us.

"Hey, Mable. Kace and Logan were married yesterday and the guys are probably still nursing hangovers." He grins.

Mable just shakes her head.

"Mable, this is Stacy. Stacy, this is Mable."

"Hey, girlie. How'd you get stuck with this one?" She points her pen toward Cole. His grin widens.

"Kidnapped," I deadpan.

Mable throws her head back and laughs. "Honey, I know several women who come here with that single hope in mind, and you sound as if it's a hardship. Cole's a nice boy," she tells me.

Boy? Cole is hardly a boy.

"Yeah, I'm a nice boy." He smirks.

"You all are. Now,"—she turns to me—"kidnapped or not, there has only been one other girl the boys have brought in here besides you, and I have it on good account that she just got married yesterday. I'm not buying it." She winks and saunters away.

I stare after her until she disappears into what I assume is the kitchen area. Turning my gaze toward Cole, I just stare at him until he elaborates.

"Just Logan." He sighs. "This is a nice place where we can come and eat and just be us. The crowd is small and most of the time, even if the patrons recognize us, they leave us alone."

"You don't bring your dates here?" Not that this is a date or anything.

He shakes his head. "I don't date, sweets. I hookup and then move on."

I cringe.

"Don't do that. Every single one of them knows the score before it happens. I make no promises. Sure, some of them think they can 'change me' or whatever, but it's just not happening."

I take a minute or two to let that sink in.

"Ya'll ready to order?" Mable asks.

Cole looks at me for confirmation, and I nod, not once having looked at the menu. "Go ahead."

He rattles off a list of breakfast foods that have my stomach growling.

"I'll just have the French toast and a glass of water, please."

"I'll have this out in a jiffy," Mable says before walking away.

"Why?" I ask, once she's gone.

"Why what?"

"Why is it that you don't want more? Why is it always just a one-time thing?" I'm not asking because I want more with him—I'm genuinely interested in why he feels that way.

Settling back against the booth, he crosses his arms over his chest. "Nothing specific or tragic in my past. I guess it's the career I've chosen. I've never been in a relationship, so to speak. I've hooked up with the same person more than once, but it was always very casual and never lasted long. There's temptation everywhere on the road. My career, what we do, women throw themselves at us. The guys and I have never had a reason not to take full advantage. The only one of us who didn't is Kacen."

"So, you're saying that if you were to be in a relationship you would cheat?" I'm trying to understand his reasoning.

"No." Uncrossing his arms, he leans in, resting them on the table. "I would never. What I'm saying is that it would take a hell of a woman to be secure enough to know that, even though there are woman throwing themselves at me, she is the only one I want. I can't imagine what it would be like if the roles were reversed, to watch guys go to the extreme to touch my girl, offer her sexual favors." His fists clench. "I don't want anyone to have to go through that. Not to mention I've yet to come across someone who I felt was worth the effort."

"The effort?" Why I keep drilling him about this, I have no idea. I can't seem to stop the words from falling from my lips. Especially since he's answering me honestly.

"Yeah, I can imagine that, when I find her, if that day ever comes, it's going to take work on my end to let her know that she's it for me. I'm not opposed to that, but I've yet to come across someone who's worth it."

His eyes bore into mine, my guess is to see if I'm offended. I'm not. We've spent time together in social situations, but never just us. Knowing if someone is worth it takes time. Time we haven't had.

"Makes sense. I see your point, but how will you ever be able to find her if you don't stop jumping from bed to bed?"

He shrugs. "Haven't really put much thought into it. It's not something I've ever imagined I would want."

"Here you go." Mable fills our table with plates of what looks like pure heaven and has my mouth watering. "I'll be right back with some refills."

"I'm starving." I reach for the syrup and drown my French toast. I can feel his eyes on me, but I don't care; I pick up my fork and take a huge bite.

"I didn't expect you to eat."

I stop, fork midair. "I'm not like all the rest." I then take my second bite of bliss. I make a mental note to give Logan a hard time for not telling me about this place.

Cole chuckles, and all conversation is lost as we devour our breakfast.

"Can I get ya'll anything else?" Mable asks.

Cole looks at me and I shake my head. "I'm stuffed."

"No, thanks, Mable. Just the check, please." He grins at her.

I reach for my purse and dig out a ten-dollar bill. Reaching out, I try to hand it to Cole, but he stares at my hand for several seconds before looking at me. "You're not paying for breakfast."

"This was not a date. I can buy my own way," I counter.

"I don't care. You're not paying. Put that away." He glares at the bill in my hand. "I'm just going to meet Mable at the counter." He slides out of the booth and walks away.

I'm not angry. In fact, it's nice that he wants to treat me to breakfast. Not necessary, but nice nonetheless. Not a very Cole-like thing to do. Then again, I don't really know him all that well, just from hanging out in group settings and from what I've learned from Logan. Instead of placing the ten back in my purse, I leave it on the table for Mable. I'm positive Cole will give her a big tip, but a little more won't hurt. After I tuck the bill underneath a plate, I slide from the booth and end up meeting Cole at the door. "Thank you," I say, looking up at him.

Reaching out, he tucks a loose strand of hair behind my ear. "You're welcome. Let's get you home." His large, warm hand settles on the small of my back as he leads me to the car.

CHAPTER 11

COLE

WHEN I DROPPED HER OFF at her apartment, she declined help with her bag. It was just a small overnight bag, so I didn't argue with her. It might not have been the most gentlemanly thing to do, but I needed to get away from her. I had planned to convince her to invite me in, maybe taste those lips again. Kacen, however, interrupted the plan. As soon as I pulled out of the diner, he texted me.

***Kacen:** Off. Limits.*

Those two words from my best friend changed my plans. He's fucking cock-blocking me from fucking Hawaii. I'll let him, until he gets back. He and I are going to have a talk. If Stacy is on board and so am I, there is no reason why the two of us—who are grown-ass adults, by the way—cannot indulge in each other. One more week and then it's game on.

"Unca Cowe!"

Crouching, I open my arms wide and wait, bracing myself for the impact of my four-year-old niece, Mia. She doesn't disappoint as she launches herself at me and wraps her arms around my neck.

"Missed you," her sweet little voice says next to my ear.

Pulling out of the hug, I stand with her in my arms, acting like she weighs a ton. "Mia, you've grown. I can barely lift you."

Her little giggles touch my heart. I love this kid something fierce. "I four now," she announces proudly.

"That's what your mom said. I might have something for you." I point to the gift bag I abandoned when I walked through the door.

"Yay!" she cheers. "I get presents fir my birfday."

"That's right. You're a big girl today," I agree with her, dropping a kiss to her cheek.

"Mia," my sister Chloe scolds her. "How many times do I have to tell you not to answer the door without an adult with you?" She stands with her hands on her hips, just like our momma used to. She really has this mom thing down.

Mia scrunches her eyebrows and looks at me. "Unca Cowe, you adult?" she asks.

I couldn't stop the grin if I tried. "Yea, Miss Mia, I'm an adult." My sister exhales loudly at my admission. "But I think what Mommy means is that you have to have someone beside you when you open the door. Was I standing beside you?" I ask her.

Sadness takes over her face as she shakes her little head. "No," she answers softly.

"Mia, remember when Mommy and Daddy talked to you about stranger danger?" Mia nods. "We want to make sure that no one ever takes you from us. It's important to wait for an adult," Chloe explains.

"Me sorry." Her lip quivers and I'm done with the conversation. I understand that she needs to learn the rules, but it's her birthday party and "Unca Cowe" can't handle the tears. She's breaking my heart.

"Hey, I heard you had a princess cake. Can I see it?" Just like that, her frown is turned upside down and her face lights up.

"Sophia. She's bewtiful," she informs me.

I let my niece drag me through the house by the hand. She jabbers on about decorations and presents and I simply follow along, letting her do her thing.

"See, Unca Cowe? Sophia." She points to the cake on the table. "Bewtiful," she says again, her eyes lighting up.

I swing her up into my arms. "You're beautiful," I tell her, which causes her to giggle. The doorbell rings and she wiggles for me to let her down. "Remember, an adult." She nods her little head and takes off running.

"You need one," my brother-in-law Kyle says from beside me.

"Why, when I can borrow yours?"

"Speaking of, I want to take Chloe out of town for a weekend. You up for uncle duties?"

"You know it. We're trying to finalize a short tour coming up in the next few months, but nothing going on really. Kacen and Logan come home tomorrow, so we'll be recording again soon. Nothing she can't be there for."

Kyle laughs. "She still talks about the last time you took her with you." He changes his voice to mimic Mia. "Unca Cowe wet me sing and it was so fun!"

"Hey, as uncle, it's my job to spoil her." I laugh at his antics. "So, when are you thinking?"

"Well, since you're open, how about next weekend? Your parents leave for the cruise this week, and mine can't get away to drive down."

"Sounds good to me. I'll make sure I stock up on some of her favorites."

"Don't tell her. I know she'll spill the beans to Chloe if she knows she gets to stay with you. I'm taking off early Friday, so I'll pick her up from daycare, pack her bag, and drop her off. My plan is to be home with mine and Chloe's bags packed as soon as she gets home."

I grip his shoulder. "Pussy."

"I'm getting it regularly," he fires back.

"Dude, that's my sister. Not to mention there is no lack of in my life."

"Yeah, that may be true." He brings his bottle of water to his lips. "But I know where mine has been."

"I get variety, and I always wrap it before I tap it."

"Don't knock it, man. You should try it sometime. You don't plan to be a bachelor forever, do you?"

I shrug. "Honestly, I don't know. I'm good with life right now. Living my dream. Who knows what could happen. But I *can* tell you that what you have with Chloe is not on my radar."

"It never is, my man. It never is."

"Daddy!" Mia comes tearing into the room. Kyle leans down and picks up his daughter. She places both of her little hands on his cheeks and kisses him. "Can we open pwesents now?" She bats her eyelashes. Damn, she's got him wrapped around her little finger.

"Let's go get Mommy," he tells her.

Figures, he's going to let Chloe be the bad cop. Not bad advice. I imagine Kacen will be the same way.

I watch as Kyle and Chloe set Mia at the head of the kitchen table, right in front of her cake. Mom has her camera, snapping pictures. Kyle lights the four candles and Mia's eyes light up. We sing "Happy Birthday" and, in her four-year-old dramatic fashion that only Mia can pull off, she blows out her candles. Mom takes over cutting the cake and passing out small plates, while Chloe and Kyle hand Mia gift after gift. She blows through them, oohing and ahhing at each one. Mine is the last, and it's something that she saw on a commercial when she was with me a few weeks ago.

"Unca Cowe! Will you haf a tea party wif me?" she asks, batting those damn eyelashes. She's wasting the cuteness on me, because there is no way I can tell that little girl no.

"You got it, Princess Mia. Go play with your friends, and we can have tea after."

"If the paparazzi could hear you now," Chloe jokes, coming to stand next to me.

"Shut it. Those fuckers make shit up anyway."

"True. She loves it. How did you know she wanted one? I expected you to call and ask for gift suggestions."

"A few weeks ago when I watched her, there was a commercial on TV. She told me she wanted it for her birfday." I chuckle. "So, I pulled it up on my laptop and ordered it."

"I'm impressed, big brother."

"Hey now, I'm more than just a pretty face." I wink at her.

"Big plans for tonight?"

I take a swig of my beer. "Yeah. Mia and I are having a tea party." I grin.

"I mean after that. Surely, Mr. Rock Star, you've got plans, ladies lining up around the corner." She sticks her finger down her throat as if she's gagging. My sister never has been fond of the . . . attention my career brings. Of course, she wants to be an aunt.

"I do, and she's this cute little thing. Brown hair, likes to wear pigtails. Today's her birthday, so we're doing it up big." I avoid looking at her, because if I do, I'll crack up laughing.

I feel a punch to my arm. "Oh, what the hell, Chloe?" I rub my arm as though she actually hurt me. She didn't, and we both know it.

"What's up with you?"

"Nothing, I promised Mia. I didn't make any plans for today because it's her birthday."

"You're acting . . . weird."

I drain my beer and set the empty bottle on the counter behind me. "I'm fine, just not feeling it tonight. Even rock stars needs downtime."

"You know I was just giving you a hard time, right?"

I can hear the concern in her voice. "Yeah, don't worry. I'm just chilling here tonight. Kacen and Logan come home tomorrow, and we're going to start tying up some loose ends on the new tracks. We've also got a few things to finalize for the tour coming up."

"How long this time?"

"Just three months. It's a short US-only tour. Kacen didn't want to do more than that, being a newlywed and all, and we all agreed. It's about making the music for us. The only reason we tour is for our fans. Don't get me wrong, it's a rush, but family's first, you know?"

"I do know. You all are a unique bunch. I'm glad that fame and fortune have not changed you. Now if I could just get you settled down. I want my nieces and nephews to be close to my kids. Mia's four."

"Hey now, just because you decided to reproduce doesn't mean I have to."

"Cole! Kyle is an only child. My aunt status depends on you."

"Sorry, sis. Hey, Kacen and Logan are gonna have one in a few months. I'll kidnap him or her periodically and you can pretend." I smirk.

"Not good enough." She stomps her foot and I throw my head back in laughter.

Kyle comes to my rescue. "Leave the poor guy alone."

"Thank you." I nod in appreciation.

"Now, we have parents who are picking up kids, and since this guy volunteered for uncle duties, you and I are going to a movie." He looks at me and I nod again.

"Go, have fun. Mia and I will hold down the fort."

Chloe grins. "You mean something besides a cartoon? Sign me up." She heads toward the backyard to start gathering kids.

"She's a handful," I say to Kyle after she's out of earshot.

"Yep, and she's my handful. Just you wait." He slaps me on the shoulder and walks off toward his wife.

CHAPTER 12

Stacy

"HELLO," I MUMBLE INTO THE phone. I have no idea what time it is, but it's still dark outside.

"Stace? Hey, it's Logan."

"Is everything all right?" I sit up in bed, rubbing the sleep from my eyes.

"Yes. Hey, listen, we're about to board our flight home, and I wanted to see if you could meet us at the house."

Squinting, I look at the clock and see that it's five forty-five in the morning. *What the hell?* "You couldn't have waited until you landed? Or sent a text maybe?" I grumble.

"Possibly, but I want you to be there when we get there. I have news," she chirps.

"Logan, I already know Kace knocked you up, and I don't need all the sexed-up details of your honeymoon. You're a married woman now."

Her infectious laugh reaches my ears through the phone line. "Shut it. Kacen and I want to talk to you about something. I'm super excited about it, and I need you to be at our place when we get there. Can you do that, Miss Moody?" she taunts.

"Moody? Really, Logan? I was sleeping!"

"Fine, I know. I'm sorry, I'm just really excited. Go back to sleep. We'll be home around five. I can't wait to see you."

Just like that, the line goes dead. How am I supposed to go back to sleep now that my mind is reeling from her "we want to talk to you" confession. UGH! I throw the covers over my head and try to clear my mind, but it's no use. Instead, I climb my tired ass out of bed and decide to go for an early-morning run.

I've kept a lot to myself this week. I've been searching for jobs online, since mine is . . . not what I originally thought. Being a drug rep sounded fun. I thought I would get to use my degree in education to teach physicians and their staff about new medications and treatment development. Instead, I get to stand at the reception window and ask for a physician's signature so I can leave samples. We do lunches for them, and even then it's as if I'm an enemy in their territory. They have to talk to me as part of the "lunch meeting," but you can tell that most of them are not the least bit thrilled about the idea.

The money is good, but I think going the traditional education route is more my speed. However, it's hard to find a job in the local school systems. Most teachers hold their positions for years, making it hard for new hires, unless someone retires.

I've been submitting my résumé to local school systems, but so far no luck. I hate the thought of staying at my current job, but even more than that, I hate the idea of moving away from my friends and family.

Logan did it. She came to Tennessee for college, met Kacen, and the rest, as they say, is history. But I would be alone, and that is not a thrilling thought.

After my run, I grab a quick shower and clean my apartment. It's weird being here all on my own. I miss my best friend.

I pass the time curled up on the couch with my Kindle. I'm so engrossed in the story that the shrill ring of my cell phone startles me. Looking down, I see it's Logan.

Shit.

"Hello," I answer, standing from the couch. I grab my purse and toss my Kindle inside, quickly grabbing my keys.

"I'm home and you're not here," she scolds me.

"I know. I'm sorry. I got engrossed in this book and lost track of time. I'm heading out now."

"Well, since it was a new book boyfriend, I'll let it go. You'll have to fill me in so I can meet him too."

Logan and I both share a love of reading. "You got it. I'll be there in twenty." I throw my phone in the cup holder, fasten my seat belt and head out. I should have told her that I was sleeping because she woke me up so damn early. I'm sure she would have loved that.

Pulling up to the gates, they open immediately, which tells me that my best friend is waiting impatiently. I take in the huge house up on the hill, and my heart bursts with happiness for her.

I park in the circular drive and, before I can even get out the car, Logan is beside the door, bouncing with excitement. "I missed you," she says, tugging on my hand to pull me from the car. Once I'm outside, she wraps her arms around me in a hug. "Come on, the guys are waiting." She pulls me toward the front door.

"The guys?" I assume she means the band, but why would they be here?

"Yeah, they're already on board." She grins.

"Logan." I pull back on her hand. "What the hell are you taking about? Already on board?"

She grins. "Come on in and we'll tell you."

I allow her to guide me into the house, still confused as to what's going on. She leads me into the living room, where Kacen, Gavin, Tristan and, of course, Cole are all gathered around. They all wave, and Cole adds a wink for good measure. I've managed to stay away from him this week. A tough feat in and of itself.

Kacen holds his hand out for Logan and she takes it, settling on his lap. "Have a seat." He motions to the empty space on the couch beside them.

"What's going on?"

Logan beams. "Well, my husband and I have been talking." Kacen kisses her temple, his hands resting on her flat belly. His smile is as wide as hers. "With the band getting ready to go on tour, he doesn't want me to have all the stress of their scheduling on my shoulders. I've assured him that I can handle it, but he read that stress is not good for me or the baby."

"I agree."

"So do we," Tristan chimes in.

"So, as my wife was saying," Kacen starts, and I can already tell these two are going to be throwing that term around a lot in the coming days. Can't say I blame them; they *are* newlyweds, after all. "I don't want her to have all this resting solely on her. I tried to convince her to give it all up, but she refused. With that being said, she has agreed to let us hire her an assistant."

"Let me get this straight. The band's assistant is going to get an assistant?" I wonder if my best friend realizes how damn lucky she is to be in the fold of these tender-hearted rockers.

"That's it exactly," Gavin confirms. "We agree with Kacen and think this is the best plan of action. Logan is still in control, since we trust her, but she gets help."

"That's a good idea, but I'm still confused as to why I need to be involved in this decision."

"Because I want you to do it," Logan explains. "I know you're not happy at your job, and it's a great chance for us to spend time together. We practically share a brain, so working so closely together won't be an issue."

Wow! Not at all what I was expecting. "I don't know how to be an assistant to a band. I have an education degree," I mumble.

"We've talked about that too," Kacen says. "When the baby gets here, I want them with me. We're only doing a short tour this time, but who knows what the future will bring. It would be nice to know that we have a private teacher for Peanut."

"Peanut?" Logan and I say at the same time.

"I refuse to call my child 'it.' Until we know the sex, I'm going with Peanut," he states firmly.

I watch as my best friend melts at his words, her lips finding his.

"I don't know." I chance a look at Cole, who's watching me intently. "Mixing business and pleasure is not always the best thing."

"We want you," Cole speaks up, and I whip my head around to face him. "Think of it as an adventure." His eyes bore into mine, almost as if his words have a double meaning. I guess, in a way, they do. He's made it clear he wants me beneath him, but if I do this, that can't happen.

I open my mouth, but no words come out.

"Just think about it. It would mean a lot to me to have you with me. The guys will be busy most of the time, and we'll get to spend a lot of time together. I miss my best friend." My earlier thoughts fall from her lips.

"Can I . . . have a few days? This is a lot to take in."

"Sure, but a few days is all we can do. If you decide against it, we need to start looking for someone else. I refuse to go on tour until we find someone," Kacen informs me.

"Come on, girl," Tristan says. "It'll be fun. You get to see a lot of new places and spend time with us." He points around the room. "What more could you ask for?" His grin is playful.

I nod. "I know. It sounds like an amazing opportunity, and I'm honored that you all would choose me, but I just need a little time to think this over. I've applied for a few teaching positions," I confess.

"Where?" Logan asks, and I can hear the worry in her voice.

I shrug. "All over, really. Just waiting to see what happens."

"We don't have that much time, and besides, Logan needs you. She's going to need her best friend in the coming months. You can't leave," Kacen says adamantly.

His plea makes me smile. He loves my best friend fiercely. "Just a couple of days."

He nods. "Okay. Now, I'm taking my wife upstairs. This is our first night in this house as husband and wife." He winks as he lifts Logan into his arms and makes good on his words. "You all can hang out or whatever, but don't plan on seeing us until tomorrow," he calls over his shoulder.

CHAPTER 13

WHEN KACE CALLED LAST NIGHT to ask my opinion of hiring Stacy to help Logan, I immediately agreed. Each point he made was valid. She's smart, we know her, and she and Logan would work great together. The teacher thing threw me for a loop, though. It's weird that he's thinking that far ahead, but I guess he has to. He's about to be a father.

Now that I'm sitting here, waiting for her to arrive so Kacen and Logan can pitch the idea, I see that it's not exactly a great thing for me—or my cock. Stacy working for the band and going on tour is just going to make us tumbling between sheets even more complicated. I've ran off an assistant or two in my day, and so have Gavin and Tristan.

I know I should let it go, but that doesn't sit well with me. I've never been one to back away from a challenge. Especially not one with legs for miles, light brown locks that feel like silk, and lips that taste like honey. Fuck, I can still remember how she tastes.

So, yeah, agreeing was not my smartest decision. All lust aside, she's a nice person, and it would be good for her to be there for Logan with the baby coming and all.

The four of us watch as Kacen carries Logan upstairs. Finally, it's

Gavin who breaks the silence. "Well, I'm headed home. Stace, I hope you accept the offer." He leans down and kisses her cheek.

I want to reach out and push him away from her. He and Tristan both know I want her. They know better.

"Thanks, Gav," she replies with a soft smile.

Gav? What the fuck? They have nicknames for each other?

"That's my vote as well. It'll be good for you to be there for Logan. We don't want all that stress on her and the baby. Not to mention the stress Kace will be under. We need you, girl." Tristan slings his arm over her shoulders and tugs her to him, giving her a hug.

I take a deep breath and exhale slowly. This is . . . different.

That same soft smile graces her lips as she looks up at him. "I'll think about it."

"Fair enough." Tristan turns to look at me. He can read me like a book; I can tell from the smirk he's now wearing. "Catch you later, C." I watch as he kisses the top of her head before releasing her.

Thank fuck they're both gone.

Stacy stares after Tristan. She's standing still, lost in thought. I quietly move forward until I'm standing right behind her. Reaching out, I gently grab her hips and pull her back against my chest.

"Think of the fun we could have," I say, my lips next to her ear. Not ten minutes ago, I was trying to talk myself out of this, but . . . I don't want to.

I can't.

"Cole." She breathes my name out, and I want to ask her to say it again. "If I take this job, that's just another reason why we can't happen."

"We're both consenting adults. We've talked about this," I remind her.

"Yes, we are. I also like to think that I'm rather responsible. Sleeping with the boss doesn't fall into that category."

"Technically, Kace is the boss. We all voted him to be the leader of the band. Your salary will be taken out of the royalties, just like ours." I move her hair to the opposite shoulder and run my nose along the length of her neck. She tilts her head to the side, giving me better access. I don't even think she realizes that she's doing it.

"We can't," she whispers as I kiss her softly at the base of her neck.

"We can. As long as we both know what the expectations are going in, it will be fine." I'm not above begging, if that's what it takes. It'll be a first for me, but this girl . . . I need her under me.

"I'm not your good-time girl, Cole."

"It would be, you know?"

"What?"

"It would be a good time. You can't deny this electricity that's between us."

"No, I'm not trying to. However, acting on it is not a good idea." She pulls out of my arms, and I miss the feel of her against me. "I'm thinking this might be a great opportunity for me, not to mention I get to work side by side with my best friend. I can't let my hormones mess that up."

I can see that war raging behind her eyes. She wants me, but she's worried. Stacy isn't like the groupies I'm used to being surrounded with. She needs to come to terms with this, with us. I'll give her the time she needs, and then I'm going to ruin her for all other men.

"I need to get going."

Reaching out, I take her hand and lace our fingers together. "I'll walk you out." She doesn't resist like I expect her to; instead, she falls into step beside me.

Once we reach her car, I open the door for her. "You got plans tonight?" She bites her bottom lip as those green eyes watch me. Lifting my hand to her chin, I gently apply pressure so she'll release her lip. I should be the only one allowed to bite them. "Don't." My voice is soft, softer than I've ever used on a woman before.

"I'm just going to grab some dinner on the way home, a drive-thru or something, and then finish the book I was reading."

"Can I take you to dinner?"

"Cole. . . ."

"We both have to eat, nothing more." I make an X across my chest. "Cross my heart." I wink.

"I don't know if that's such a great idea."

"Sure it is. I can answer any questions you may have about being on the road and what our everyday lives are like. I'm sure Logan tells you a lot, but this is coming from a band member. Get the scoop so you can make an informed decision."

I can tell that my excuse has her. She's going to say yes. And I'm more excited about that than I should be.

"Okay, but nothing else. I'll follow you." She steps toward the open door of her car.

"I can drive us," I offer.

"No, really, it's fine. I'll just follow you there."

"Fine. At least give me your number in case we get separated, so I can reach you."

She's reluctant, but when I hand her my phone, she types in her contact information. I want to fist bump at this breakthrough. Instead, I smile, waiting for her to get in the car and buckle up. Once she's strapped in, I shut the door and jog to my truck. She's making me work for it, but it's . . . fun. It's been a while coming for us. She thinks she's keeping me at bay, when really she's just making the chase that much more exciting.

CHAPTER 14

Stacy

MY PALMS ARE SWEATY AS I grip the wheel. What the hell was I thinking? I never should have agreed to dinner. It was those brown eyes that captivated me. That and it really would be nice to get an inside look at what it's like being on the road. Logan can try to convince me all she wants, but the reality of the situation is that she really has no clue. This will be a first for her as well. She *does* have the advantage of being married to the lead singer; me, I'm just the tagalong best friend.

I've read the tabloid headlines. Do I want to live the life of a rock star? Do I want to be engrossed in that world? I know because of my association with Logan that I will be a little bit regardless, but being on tour with the band and hanging out with my best friend at her house with the band members is two totally different things. This is not an easy decision to make.

Cole taps his brakes and hits his turn signal. It's not until we're in the lot that I realize we're at a Subway. I can't help but grin. The famous Cole Hampton rolling up in a Subway to order dinner. It's so hard to see them as normal, everyday people, but I have to admit they don't live the catered life you think of when you think rock star.

Cole appears at my door and pulls it open. Reaching out, he offers me his hand. Hesitantly, I place my hand in his and he helps me from the car.

"This place looks dead tonight, and they're cool."

"Cool?" I ask.

"Yeah. Me and the guys come here a lot. The staff is used to us and they respect our privacy. They don't tweet it out and ask for pictures. They let us be . . . normal."

"That's good that you have that here, close to home."

"Yeah, it's rough on the road."

Before I can reply, his hand is on the small of my back and he's leading me inside.

"Hey, Mr. Hampton," a teenage boy behind the counter greets us.

"Tommy, enough with the Mr. Hampton. That's my dad. Just Cole, my man." He holds out a fist and the kid, with a blush on his face, connects his to Cole's.

"Go ahead and order, sweets." His deep timbre causes me to shiver.

"Uh, I'll take . . . um, a six-inch turkey on wheat," I stumble through my order. After I tell him what I want, Cole suggests I find us a table. I look around the empty room and then back at Cole. He simply grins and winks. "Here." I hand him some money.

"Not happening, babe. We've had this talk and we can have it again, but it's going to be the same outcome. Besides, I asked you here. My treat. Now, find us a spot and settle in, because I've got to educate you about life on the road."

Not wanting to make a scene—not to mention it would be pointless because Cole is not the type to give in on this kind of thing—I politely thank him and grab our drinks. I pick a table at the very back of the restaurant. Hopefully, it stays slow, but if not, this should give us some semblance of privacy.

"I'm an open book," Cole says, sliding into the booth across from me. He passes me my sandwich and a bag of chips.

"Thank you."

He nods as he takes the first bite—if that's what you want to call it. He looks like a chipmunk.

"I don't really know where to start," I confess. "Maybe you can just tell me about what goes on. What's a normal day like?"

"It's really just us guys hanging out. None of us have ever brought a girl on tour, so it's going to be different this time. We all love Logan like a sister, and she makes Kace happy, but it's just going to be different."

"She's going to cramp your style," I tease him.

His grin lights up his face, and I find myself wanting to make him smile like this more often. He really is easy on the eyes.

"No, she will not cramp our style. We don't bring girls on the bus, which is a rule we've all had. None of us wants to hear one of the others getting their rocks off."

I choke on my water. "Well, okay then."

"Being on the road is more than just singing a few songs and getting laid. This is a shorter tour, so it's jam-packed with back-to-back concerts in different cities. We have radio spots, and I think there's even a television appearance on the books."

"So, why exactly do you need me?"

"Logan's pregnant." He says it like I should know from just those two words.

"And? Women have been having babies for a while now." I smirk.

"Ha ha, smartass. Dealing with schedules, the label, venues—it can all get pretty stressful. We talked about it, and none of us want all that pressure on Logan. We figured we would hire someone to split the duties, take some of the pressure off."

"I'm a teacher. Not sure how my education and experience will benefit the band."

He shrugs. "Kace is a planner, always has been. Sounds like he expects this to be a permanent thing. Once the baby gets older, I assume they'll hire someone to replace you and let you tutor."

I'm surprised at his candid answers. Not only that, but he seems to understand Kacen. "That's jumping the gun a little, don't you think?"

"Maybe, maybe not. I know Kacen will refuse to travel without either of them." He studies me for a few minutes, as if he needs to gather his thoughts. "The guys and I have always said if one of us wants out, then we're all done. It's something we started together, and it's something we will end together. I see you as Kacen's way of making sure his family has the best of what it needs. Logan gets her best friend, and their kid gets a good teacher—when the time comes, of course."

"I guess I can see that. It's just hard to believe he would be thinking so far ahead."

"Like I said, Kacen is a planner. He's not like the rest of us. He never was about hooking up and living the lifestyle to the stereotype that it is. He's always just wanted to find that one person who gets him and have a family. He found that with Logan, and he won't stop until he gives her and this baby the world."

His words shouldn't surprise me, and they don't really. I know this about my best friend's husband. He loves her fiercely. He's why I've changed my ways. I don't see the point in wasting my time with guys where I see no future; I want what Logan and Kacen have. That's why I must avoid Cole's advances. Well, that and the fact that I'm afraid it will be awkward as hell, and who wants to deal with that?

"And what about you, Tristan and Gavin? Do you live up to the stereotype?" I settle back against my seat, prepared for him to backpedal his way out of answering.

"We do." He nods. "Women throw themselves at you for doing what you love. We're all three single and unattached, so we take advantage of what's offered. None of us give them false hope that it will ever be more. We never do repeats and yes, before you ask, we have run off an assistant or two."

"I appreciate your honesty. I'm a little surprised, actually."

"Don't be. With me, what you see is what you get. I have nothing to hide. I'm not ashamed of how I've lived my life to this point. I'm living every man's fantasy."

"You're really okay with that? A different girl in each city, never having an emotional connection?"

"Oh, sweetheart, it's emotional. Trust me."

"You know what I mean." I want to tell him that I've thought in extreme detail more than once how "emotional" things could be between us.

"I don't think I do," he admits.

"Someone to wake up to every day. Someone to lie next to at night. That one person who knows you inside and out, your crutch through life."

"I have the guys, and I have my family."

"Yeah, but the intimacy isn't there." My cheeks heat as I think of how to get my point across in a way that he might understand. "I want to know that when I fall apart at a man's touch, that he's also going to be the one there to catch me when I fall in life, not just in the bedroom. I want a lover and a best friend."

I watch as he thinks about what I've just said. "It's not something I've ever wanted or thought about, really. When I was younger, it wasn't on my radar because, like most teenage boys, I thought with my cock. Once we signed with the label and released the first album, we kind of blew up overnight. Women were all over us, and I never looked back."

"That must be lonely."

"Nah, the variety keeps it interesting." He wags his eyebrows at me, and I can't stop the laughter from falling from my lips.

"Okay, funny man, you know that's not happening. Tell me more about being on the road." We spend the next two hours sitting in the back booth of Subway, talking about life on tour. Cole is open and honest, just as he said he would be. To my surprise, life on the road is not just one big party.

"Umm, Mr. Hampton—I mean Cole. We're closing now," Tommy says from beside us.

This causes me to look at my watch. "It's late. Sorry for overstaying our welcome." I smile at Tommy.

He blushes. "No, you didn't, it's just time to close."

"Thanks, man. See you next time." Cole stands, reaching out for me. This is starting to become a habit, one that I refuse to admit I enjoy. He walks me to my car. "Thanks for eating with me. I hope you take the job." He tucks a loose piece of hair behind my ear. "It will be good for Logan to have you around."

He says it will be good for Logan, but the heat in his eyes tells me that he's not over the idea of the two of us taking a roll in his satin sheets. "I'll think about it. Thank you for taking the time to answer my questions."

"Drive safe, sweets." He opens my door and waits for me to settle in before closing it and tapping twice on the hood.

Slowly, I back out of the lot. In the rearview mirror, I see that he watches me drive away.

CHAPTER 15

I'M SITTING ON KACEN'S FRONT steps, waiting for Kyle to drop Mia off, when Stacy pulls up. I've left her alone these last few days. I know she was trying to make her decision, and me and my cock needed to stay out of that equation. She needed to make the best choice for her, and then I would pick up my game. Logan informed us that she called and asked if she could come over to give us her decision. Now, here she is.

"Do you ever go home?" she asks as she climbs the steps.

I pat the concrete beside me, inviting her to sit. To my surprise, she does. "I go home, but Kacen has a studio here, and we're rehearsing for the tour," I remind her.

"Right. So, what are you doing sitting out her all by yourself?"

"Waiting on my niece. My brother-in-law surprised my sister with a weekend away, and I get to watch the munchkin."

Her mouth falls open as she stares at me.

"What?"

"You babysit? How old is she?"

"Yes, I babysit. I'm a kick-ass uncle, thank you very much. Mia's four."

"You continue to surprise me, Cole Hampton."

I can tell she's having a hard time seeing me as a caretaker for a four-year-old little girl. "I'm more than a pretty face with hands that were made to caress the strings of a guitar." I wink then stand when I see Kyle's truck pass the gates. Stacy sits quietly on the steps, taking it all in.

"Unca Cowe!" Mia's little feet fly across the driveway. I bend down just in time to catch her. "My daddy says I get to stay wif you. Hims is takin Mommy on a date." She grins.

I kiss the top of her head—she's too fucking cute. "I know, and that means you and I get to have a sleepover all weekend."

"Yay! Are the boys here?" she asks. I chuckle at her calling my bandmates "boys."

"Yeah, they're here. We're going to hang out for a little bit and then we can go to my place."

"Here's her bag. Thanks, man," Kyle says, setting the pink princess bag at my feet.

"No problem, my man. Enjoy your weekend."

"Oh, I plan to. Mia needs a baby brother." He smirks.

"Yes!" Mia exclaims. Suddenly, she notices Stacy sitting on the step. "Who are you?" she asks.

Stacy stands. "I'm a friend of the boys and Logan."

"Logan! Is she here, Unca Cowe? She always pways wif me."

"Logan lives here now, so yes, she's here."

"Yay! Bye, Daddy." She leans over and kisses her dad on the cheek.

Kyle just chuckles at his daughter. "Be good, princess. I love you."

"Bye, Daddy." Mia smiles and waves.

"All right, little miss, let's get you inside. Have you had dinner?" I ask her.

"Nope, but Daddy let me have some cookies." She didn't need to tell me, as she's still wearing the evidence.

"Let me guess." I tap my finger against my chin. "Chocolate chip?"

Mia gasps. "How did you know?" Her eyes are wide with wonder.

"It's nice to meet you, Mia. I'm Stacy." She holds her hand out. Mia mimics her and they shake hands.

"Can we be fwiends?"

Stacy beams at her, and I have to think about anything but her. It's awkward for your cock to get hard when you're holding your four-year-old niece.

"I would love that, Princess Mia."

Stacy reaches down and grabs her bag; I nod my thanks and pull open the door. I motion with my head for Stacy to go in. "Ladies first," I tell her.

"'Cause wadies are pwincesses," Mia adds. I love this little girl.

I catch the grin Stacy is wearing as she slides in front of me and into the house. As soon as I cross the threshold, Mia is squirming to get down. Once her feet hit the floor, she's making a mad dash for the living room.

"She's something else," Stacy says.

"That she is." I grab her hand and pull her with me into the living room. We get there just in time to watch Kacen intercept Mia before she launches herself at Logan.

"Kacen!" Mia giggles as he tickles her.

Once she settles down, Kacen carries her to the couch and sits next to Logan. "I have a secret," he says in a quiet voice.

Mia blinks and nods, hanging on his every word.

"Logan and I got married. Did you know that?"

Mia nods that yes, she did know.

"Well, now that we're married, we get to have a baby." He points to Logan's belly.

Mia's eyes, still wide, stare at Logan's belly for the longest time. Then she raises her head, her gaze locked on Logan's. "You have a baby in there?" she whispers.

"I do." Logan is so fucking happy it radiates from her and Kacen both.

"Wow. I need to tell my mommy and daddy. Daddy said I need a wittle bwother."

Kacen turns his head, burying his face in his shoulder to keep from laughing.

Mia turns to me. "Unca Cowe, you need to get mawied."

I grin. "I do?"

She nods. "Uh-huh.

"Why's that?"

"'Cause we need more babies." Her expression tells me that, to her, this is not a joking matter.

I walk to the couch and bend my knees so she and I are eye to eye. "Mia, you only get married if you love the person so very much that you can't breathe without them. I haven't found her yet, but when I do, I'll let you know." Who am I to crush her dreams that good old Unca Cowe doesn't have any plans for weddings and babies in his future? My sister would have my balls if I ruined her fantasies about happily ever after.

"Mia, do you think you could help me and Stacy make some dinner? I was thinking spaghetti," Logan asks her.

"My favowite!" And just like that, she's jumping off Kacen's lap and reaching for Stacy's hand, which surprises all of us. "Do you have a baby in your belly too?" she asks.

"No, sweetie. I'm not married," Stacy explains gently.

Mia looks up at me, her smile a mile wide. "Unca Cowe, you can marry her." She stands tall and proud as if she just solved world peace—not that she knows what that is.

I want to tell her that I don't want to marry the lovely Stacy, but I do ache to burry my cock deep inside her. Instead, I go with, "I'm starving."

"Skettie!" she cheers and pulls Stacy to the kitchen, Logan trailing behind them.

I'm thankful that her four-year-old brain can switch topics so easily.

"You ready for that, man?" I ask Kacen.

"Hell yes." No hesitation what so ever.

"Where are Gavin and Tristan?"

"In the studio. Tristan was working on his solo beat. Gav was just hanging out on his phone."

"Let's go see what Tristan and his sticks have come up with. Fucking drumming genius."

"Wait." He reaches out and grabs my arm. "With the distraction of Mia, I didn't get to ask Stacy what her answer is. I can't wait any longer to see if she's taking the job. I really want it to be her with Logan." He turns toward the kitchen and I follow behind him.

I'm torn. I want her to take the job—it's a great opportunity to travel, and she'll get to do it with her best friend—but I still want to fuck her. Her taking the job is going to make that even more difficult.

"Stacy, you said you made a decision?" Kacen asks.

Lifting her head from the salad she and Mia are making, she smiles softly. "Yeah, I did. I'd like to accept the position. I'm nervous I'll mess something up, but I'm excited. Thank you for the opportunity, Kacen . . . Cole." Her eyes lock on mine.

Fuck me, she said yes.

"Unca Cowe, you wanna help?" Mia asks.

I'm just about to tell her that I can't when Kacen chimes in. "What about me? I'm an excellent cook." He leans on the counter in front of where Mia is standing on a chair.

"Kace, you funny." Mia giggles. It's not until I see Kacen's face that I understand her laughter. He has a mouth full of cooked spaghetti noodles hanging out of his mouth.

"I thought you were cooking for me?" I ask Mia.

"I not you wife." She puts her little hand on her hip, and I can see my sister's attitude shining through.

"But you're my favorite girl," I tell her.

Mia gives off a heavy sigh. "Fine, you can haf some."

I grin and reach for the bowl of noodles only to have my hand smacked away. Logan smirks at me.

It's not until I see Mia dig her little hands in and flip the noodles around that I understand. Logan is pouring more noodles into a boiling pot; this is Mia's bowl to "cook" with.

"Wook, Stacy." Mia holds up two hands full of noodles. "I make skettie."

"Look at you. You're doing a great job, Mia."

"Mia, did I tell you that I bought some new puzzles? I was hoping you would stop by so we could put them together," Logan tells her.

"Yay!" Mia throws her hand up and slings noodles on Kacen and me.

"Oh, no, now you're going to get it," I tell her, raising my hands. "You know what this means, right, Mia?" She's already giggling so hard she can't speak and I haven't even touched her yet.

"The t-tickle mo-monster," she sputters out.

I quickly stand and gather her under my arm, pretending to fly her around the kitchen. "Attention, passengers, please prepare for a crash tickle landing," I say in a cheesy announcer voice.

"Unca Cowe!" Mia laughs. I love this little girl.

I take off toward the living room and we do a crash landing on the couch. I immediately let the tickling commence. Mia shrieks and writhes.

"Stop, pwease! Pretty pwease," she begs.

I stop since she said the magic words. She sits up, catches her breath, and then throws her arms around my neck. "I wuv you, Unca Cowe."

I'm a man. I like manly things like sports and drinking a few cold ones with the guys. I don't do relationships and I enjoy female company—lots of it. However, in the presence of my four-year-old niece, I lose my damn man card.

I return her hug. "Love you, too, Mia."

I hear a throat clearing. *Great, busted.* I look up to find Stacy standing there, taking in all in. I should be embarrassed, but I'm not. I'm not a monster who is incapable of love; I just choose to have variety in my life instead.

"Dinner's ready," she tells us. "Mia, your noodles look delicious," she adds with a wink. I'm positive that's her way of telling me that we won't be eating Mia's noodles.

"Let's go munchkin. Time to eat some skettie." I stand with Mia in my arms and carry her to the kitchen. Logan pulls out a booster seat from the pantry, and I raise my eyebrows in question.

She waves me off. "I like when Mia comes to visit."

Nothing else is said as I get Mia set up in the chair beside mine and we settle in to eat. Mia drives the conversation. She has the full attention of all six of us.

CHAPTER 16

THE LAST TWO MONTHS HAVE been crazy. Logan and Cassidy, the assistant to the band's manager, Mr. Jones have been training me. Between the two of them, they have been giving me a crash course on all things in the music industry. I can now see why Kacen didn't want all this pressure on his pregnant wife—holy shit, there's a lot to do. The logistics alone are a nightmare. Cassidy assures us that she will be helping from the home office as well.

I've managed to avoid Cole and his sexiness. I see him in passing, but never allowing enough time for conversation or flirting. I may be telling him no, but he's still the one starring in my dreams late at night. Bob, my battery operated boyfriend, and I have become close thanks to Cole Hampton.

"Are you all packed?" I ask Logan.

"Gah! No, I don't even know how to pack for three months."

"Tell me about it."

"Kacen says not to worry about it, that we can buy anything we need. I'm just not used to this, you know?"

"I know, but he's right. You're going to need maternity clothes." I wink.

"Yes." She holds her arm out. "Pinch me."

"What?" I laugh at her because she's lost her damn mind.

"I said pinch me. Is this real? Is this really my life?"

"Yes and yes. Get used to it. That man is never letting you go."

"Yeah." She wears a blissful smile that I once again find myself envious of.

"Are you excited for the stop in Ohio?"

"I am. It will be nice to stay in our house there. Get a break from the bus."

"This is either going to be the best or the worst three months of our lives."

"I know. I worry, though. What if I hate it? Kacen will never tour again."

"Just give it a fair shot. Besides, from what I understand, the guys all know this is what Kacen wants. If one wants out, they all do."

She looks surprised. "You have a good informant."

"Cole and I had dinner the night you offered me the job. He filled me in on what happens out on the road. That was a part of our conversation."

"He still trying to get you into his bed?"

"He's been quiet the last couple of months. My guess is because they've been rehearsing like crazy for the tour. Not to mention I've been nose-deep trying to learn the ropes."

"He's not one to give up easily."

"I can hold him off. I've done it this long."

"I don't know, Stacy. Maybe you should give it a shot. You could be his game-changer."

I throw my head back in laughter. "Cole Hampton doesn't have a desire to change the game. He's living the dream. From his lips to my ears," I tell her.

"He's just caught up in the routine. He needs something to mix it up, needs to see what he's missing. Cole's a great guy who just needs the right woman to keep him on his toes."

"Let me guess, you think that woman is me?"

Logan smiles. "Maybe. You never know. You can try. Worst-case scenario, it doesn't work out."

"Heartbreak."

"Yeah, but what's that saying? 'Better to have loved and lost than to never love at all.'"

"Says the girl who is blissfully married to her best friend."

"You're my best friend."

"I am, but so is he, in a more intimate way."

Her hands fall over her barely-there baby bump. "I'm having a baby."

"You are. You'll have, what? A month left by the time the tour is over?"

"Yes, Kacen is still freaking out about it. The doctor has assured him that it's fine."

"He's going to be such a good daddy," I gush.

"He is. He already has a crew on standby to start the nursery once we find out the sex."

"I can't wait to start shopping. I think we should pick something up in each city for Peanut."

"I think that's a great idea." We both startle at Kacen's words. "Sorry, didn't mean to sneak up on you. You all packed, baby?"

The three of us look at the pile of clothes still lying on the bed. "Uh . . . getting there," Logan tells him.

"I can see that. The guys are all going to stay here tonight. The bus is supposed to be here at eight. Stacy, you might as well stay too. Grab your things and bring them over. That way, we all get a good night's sleep and no one has to get up at the ass-crack of dawn."

"I can do that. Thank you." I finish folding the shirt in my hands. "I think I'll head over. I have some packing to finish as well. I'll be back in a few hours."

"Stacy," Logan calls my name just as I reach the door. "Thank you. I don't think I could do this"—she points to her belly—"on the road without you. Thank you."

"It's an amazing opportunity. I should be thanking both of you." With that, I give them a small wave and head to my apartment that just so happens to be over my parents' garage. As I get closer, excitement takes over. It's the best of both worlds—I get to travel the world with people I know and care about.

Soul Serenade "Making Love" Tour, here I come.

CHAPTER 17

COLE

I SPENT LAST NIGHT AT my sister's. Mom and Dad come over and we just hung out. Chloe and Kyle announced a few weeks ago that they're expecting baby number two. My sister was beaming with happiness, as was Kyle. That seems to be my world lately. Marriage, babies . . . love. I'm happy for all of them, but I'm putting my energy into the tour.

None of us has mentioned it, but this could very well be our last, at least for a while. Lives are changing and we made a pact, which I think is why I'm so stoked for this one. It's only three months, and US only. I prefer that if I'm being honest; international travel is exhausting.

We would still write and make music, but touring could be too much with families. Something the four of have always agreed on is that family comes first, always. Music will be there, but nothing can replace those you love.

The cab pulls up to the gate and I punch in my code. We're all staying here tonight, which is our normal routine before hitting the road. We can sleep in and get a good night's rest.

The cab stops next to another just like it. It's not until I'm climbing out that I see it's her.

Stacy.

That's when I'm reminded that she's going to be sleeping under the same roof as me tonight. Sleeping on the same bus for the next three months. Kacen gave me a lecture a few days ago. "She's not someone to mess with, Cole," he had said. Like I don't know that. I know she's one of the good ones. The Logans and Stacys of the world deserve more than just to be worked over in a night of passion. I know that, but that doesn't change the fact that my cock and I still want her.

I quicken my stride to take her bags from the cabbie. "I got it, man."

"Thank you, Cole."

The way she says my name with her slight southern accent has my cock twitching, thinking it's time to come out and play. It's going to be a long three months if I can't get this girl under me.

"You ready to make love?" I ask with a smirk on my face.

Her cheeks instantly redden. "Cole, we've. . . ."

"The tour, sweets. Are you ready for the Soul Serenade 'Make Love' Tour?" I ask with as much innocence as I can muster.

Her face glows with her embarrassment. "Oh, um . . . Yeah, I guess. As ready as I'll ever be."

Leaning down, my lips find her ear. "You were thinking about me. Thinking about us. I'm not one for making love, but I can guarantee that you'll beg for more."

To my surprise, her body relaxes into mine. My words affect her.

"Whenever you're ready, you let me know." I kiss just below her ear and can see the goose bumps break out over her skin. With extreme strength, and a rock-hard cock, I step away from her, grab both of our bags and head inside.

The foyer is filled with luggage; I add ours to the mix and follow the voices into the living room. Tristan and Gavin are sitting on the couch, legs propped up on the table. Kacen and Logan are curled up together in the oversized chair. That leaves the love seat, and I give an internal fist bump; Stacy is going to have to sit beside me.

"Hey, man," Tristan says.

I nod in greeting. "What are we watching?"

The four of them look at me, all wearing confused looks.

"Seriously, none of you know?"

Gavin and Tristan both have their phones in their hands and Kacen has his wife in his. I just shake my head and reach for the remote. "Stacy's here too. My cab pulled up just after hers."

"This is really happening," Logan says, her voice reverent.

"It's happening, baby," Kacen tells her.

"Hey, you all packed?" Logan asks Stacy as she enters the room.

I watch as she surveys the area, looking at the couch where Gav and Tristan are sprawled out. I purposely made sure there looked like plenty of room was left on the love seat beside me. I can change that once she decides to sit down. She glances at the spot beside me and she looks nervous. I flash her a calming smile and I can see the minute her decision is made.

"Yes, I just brought the basics," she tells her best friend as she moves toward me.

As soon as she sits, I shift a little closer. I don't think she notices. This girl—what is it about her that I can't let go? It has to be the chase. The fact that she doesn't fall at my feet like all the others. I didn't realize how fun it could be to pursue someone.

Stacy settles back against the couch, and I lift my arm and lay it across the back. I'm not touching her, but it's a more intimate position for sure. Logan gives us a bright smile, while Kacen looks worried. Gavin and Tristan are oblivious, lost in whatever it is on their phones that's captured their attention.

"What are we watching?" Stacy asks.

I chuckle and hand her the remote. "They have no idea." I roll my eyes.

"You pick." She passes it back to me.

"I'm good with anything." I gently touch her arm and push. It's not lost on me that I really want to be pulling her into my lap and crushing her lips with mine. Patience is not something I've had to practice, since our careers make it possible to have what we want at our fingertips. Until now, that is.

She scrolls through the channels, not finding anything.

"Wait, go back," Logan says. I didn't even realize she was paying attention.

Stacy backs through the channels. "There." Logan grins. *Pretty Woman* is playing. "I love this movie."

Satisfied, Stacy sets the remote on the table in front of us. I kick off my shoes and prop my feet up.

I couldn't care less what movie the girls want to watch, since I doubt I'll be able to pay much attention anyway. Instead, I'll be sitting here, breathing in her sweet scent. Mentally arguing with my cock that it's not time to come out and play. I want it just as bad as he does, maybe more, but I need to spend some time getting to know her better. Figure out a way to convince her that a night together would not be a mistake.

As the sun sets, the house grows dark, with only the TV for light. Gavin has fallen asleep. Tristan goes back and forth from the movie to his phone. Kacen only has eyes for his wife, and her eyes are glued to the screen. Stacy is just as engrossed. She wiggles in her seat, and I let instinct take over. My arm, which has been stretched out on the back of the love seat, drops to her shoulders and I pull her against me. She doesn't resist like I assumed she would; instead, she looks up from under her lashes, those big green eyes questioning me.

"Relax," I whisper. She continues to watch me, searching for an ulterior motive. She must find what she's looking for. Her eyes leave mine and focus back on the movie as she settles against me.

That's when it hits me—I've never done this. I'm twenty-five years old and I've never just hung out with a girl. Never just held anyone in my arms for the sake of watching a movie. Well, no one but Mia. I admit that it's . . . relaxing. No pressure, no pretense—just chilling on the couch, beautiful girl in my arms.

CHAPTER 18

I'M TOO TIRED TO ARGUE with him. That look, it was like he was trying to tell me not to overthink this. I'm not going to. Instead, I will my body to relax against his. He's hard, defined, yet soft. The minute his strong arms wrap around me, I sigh. This is a side of Cole I've never seen. I know he's been with women since I've known him, but I've never once seen him show this type of . . . affection. I guess that's not a part of the deal—you don't have to cuddle to get off.

I chance a look around the room and no one is paying us a bit of attention, which has me relaxing further into his embrace. I miss this part of being in a relationship.

I clear my mind of the sexy beast who has his arms around me and focus on the movie. I don't know how much time goes by before Cole shifts his weight, turning his body toward mine. His strong arms pull me closer, my head now resting against his chest. His heart is beating a steady rhythm, his hand is trailing gently up and down my back, and I find it hard to keep my eyes open.

"Stop," I hear Cole say in a low but firm voice.

"Cole," Kacen warns.

"Let her be," Cole replies.

"Are you sure?" Logan asks.

"I got her. You all go on to bed."

I know they're talking about me. I also know I should wake up and put an end to the disagreement, but I just can't. My body is warm and relaxed, so instead, I nuzzle closer to him before sleep claims me once again.

When I wake again, the house is dark and quiet. I open my eyes and let them adjust to the darkness. I'm lying on top of Cole, his arms clamped tight around me as he sleeps what I assume is peacefully, based on the gentle rise and fall of his chest. I wish I could see him, that I could commit this moment with him and what he looks like to memory. Damn the darkness.

I lie as still as I can, just soaking up his warmth. Pretending this is any other man. Pretending he's not a famous musician and that we could be on our way to something real. I know it's dangerous to even contemplate it for a second, but Cole is one of those magnetic personalities. He's crude one minute and apparently cuddly the next. He's a lethal combination that I cannot let myself long for. I want it all, and he wants one night.

Coming to my senses, I slowly start to pull away, but his arms tighten.

"I got you," his deep, raspy, sleep-laced voice cuts into the night.

"We need to go to bed."

"I'm good here." He still has his arms gripped like a vice around me.

"Cole, come on," I plead with him. I would love nothing more than to settle against his chest and fall back to my fantasy of him, or better yet take him up to the guest room and have him crawl in bed behind me. All fantasies that I can't allow myself to indulge in.

"Cole, let me up."

"Fine," he grumbles, but releases me.

I crawl off him and stand beside the love seat. Cole follows suit, his hands resting on my hips. "I'll guide you," he says softly.

I nod, even though he can't see me. Stepping in front of me, he laces his fingers through mine and we begin to slowly move toward the stairs. He knows his way around in the darkness. I could insist that we turn on a light, or hell, even use the light on my cell phone, but instead, I continue pretending that I need him just to feel his hand in mine. Pathetic, I know, but I'm just not ready to let go of the fantasy.

He slowly climbs the stairs, keeping a firm grip on my hand. We reach the top and he leads me down the hall. We finally stop in front of what I assume is my room.

"You want me to come with you?" he asks, his voice husky.

YES! "No, get some rest. Sorry about tonight."

His hands find my cheeks in the dark. "Don't apologize, sweets. I enjoyed every minute of it." I know he's close, but due to the dark of night, I have no warning that his lips are headed for mine until I feel them, firm yet soft. My brain is still caught up in the fantasy that I created when I woke up, foggy from wanting him. My hands find his long hair and my fingers bury deep, pulling him closer. He doesn't disappoint as he deepens the kiss.

When he steps in to me, I back up and my back hits the door. Cole's lips never leave mine. Slowly, softly, he devours me, if that's even possible. He gently traces my lips with his tongue, and I don't hesitate to open for him. He groans as his hands tilt my head just where he needs it. And we kiss, for I don't know how long. He doesn't take it further, and neither do I; instead, I enjoy the weight of his body pressed against mine, the feel and the taste of his lips. This is my one moment of weakness before the three-month adventure ahead of us. In the back of my mind, I know it's a bad idea, but I can't find the will to care at the moment.

Finally, he slows the kiss and rests his head on my shoulder. "Good night, sweet Stacy." His voice is gruff and low. Reaching behind me, he grabs the handle and pushes open the door.

I turn on shaking legs and dip under his arm. "Night, Cole," I say softly into the darkness. He doesn't reply as he shuts the door.

Just like that, the fantasy is over.

Blindly, I find my way to the bed. Climbing in, I burrow under the covers and will sleep to claim me. I lie there in the darkness for what feels like hours before exhaustion finally takes over. However, sleep doesn't stop the memories of his lips, his body pressed to mine, from appearing in my thoughts.

What was I thinking?

CHAPTER 19

NO FUCKING WAY I CAN sleep after that. After cuddling with her, holding her while she slept, kissing her. She affects me like no one before her. I don't quite know what it means or how to handle it. The entire night is like a movie reel behind my eyes, playing on repeat, and I lie awake, remembering every second over and over again. The sun begins to rise and I feel a ping of excitement that I'll be seeing her in just a couple of hours. The bus rolls out early, so the quiet house is soon to be bustling with the six of us preparing to leave. Just the thought motivates me to shower and change.

I hesitate in the hall by her door, but make myself keep walking. I find Logan in the kitchen, sitting on the counter while drinking orange juice.

"Morning," I say, making my way toward the coffeemaker. I need caffeine after my sleepless night.

"Morning. You look tired."

Logan misses nothing when it comes to us. "Yeah, didn't sleep the best."

"That love seat is too small for you," she scolds me.

"It is," I agree. "But she was sleeping too peacefully to wake her up."

She raises her eyebrows, silently questioning me.

"We woke up at some point in the middle of the night. I made sure she got to her room safely and then went to mine." *After I kissed the fuck out of her.*

"I see." She smirks.

I ignore her and continue making coffee. She's dying to ask me, and I'm actually surprised that she's being so reserved—everyone knows I'm an open book.

Logan sits on the counter and quietly drinks her juice, which gets to me more than the questioning. "Say it," I finally spit out, no longer able to handle the silence.

"That's a first for you," she replies matter-of-factly.

I don't bother playing dumb; I know what she means, and it *was* a first for me. "We were both comfortable, no point in moving."

"Yeah, I get that. That's a first in itself, but you hanging out with a girl, just to hang out? That, too, is a first."

Dammit. "Yeah."

"And?" she pries for more.

"And what?" I know what she wants, but it's fun to see her get irritated with me.

"How was it?" she probes.

Finally, the coffee is done. I pour my first cup—straight-up black and strong, just want I need. "I can see the merit," I answer honestly. This, of course, has Logan beaming.

"That's not exactly the answer I was expecting."

"Sorry to disappoint you," I say mockingly, and she shoves my arm. "Hey now, hot coffee here."

"I woke up alone." Kacen literally pouts as he walks into the kitchen. He doesn't stop until he's standing in front of Logan and kisses her good morning.

"So, wheels up in, what? An hour?" I ask.

"We're not flying," Gavin says, plopping down in a chair at the table.

"I know that, ass munch. It's a figure of speech."

"Coffee, I need coffee." Tristan heads for the coffeepot behind me. I step aside, letting him get his caffeine fix.

"Where's Stacy?" Kacen asks, his jaw tense.

"I assume she's in her room, where I left her last night once we both woke up." I know he's worried, but he's got to ease up. I know after last night more than ever that she and I will have our chance. It will be a night to remember for both of us, and it's going to happen. She's just too damn sweet.

"Good morning." That voice belongs to the girl who kept me up last night.

"Hey, you ready for this?" Logan asks her.

"Ready as I'll ever be. Coffee?" she inquires.

I grab Tristan's arm and move him to my other side. He's still half asleep so he doesn't protest.

"Cream and sugar?" I ask her. She has yet to look at me, but my question forces her to do so.

"Um, no, just black. I can get it."

Reaching into the cabinet, I pull down another mug. I almost hand her mine, but I don't think I can take seeing her lips where mine have been—it's too soon for that. I pour her a cup and hand it to her.

"Thank you," she says as our fingers touch. I feel that gentle brush of her fingers . . . everywhere.

"The bus will be here in thirty minutes. Everyone packed up?" Kacen asks.

We all nod and mumble our answers. I'm about to spend three months on a tour bus with a girl who tempts me, who has done nothing but occupy my mind for the last several weeks. Who am I kidding—I've wanted her since the minute I laid eyes on her.

This should be interesting.

CHAPTER 20

THE BUS IS LOADED AND we're just waiting on the guys to join us. Logan and I are sitting at the small U-shaped dining table. My hands are resting on my lap, palms sweaty as what I'm about to do sinks in. I'm traveling with Soul Serenade. That's a lot to wrap your head around.

It's really happening.

"This is a new bus. I guess the old one only had bunks, and Kacen insisted we have a bed." Logan places a hand over her belly.

"That's a good man you married," I say with a smile.

"He really is. Anyway, there is a bedroom in the back and then four bunks, a full bathroom and this living area that you see."

"You've seen the bus before?" I ask her.

"Just plans and pictures. This is my first time being onboard. The guys designed it."

"It's not exactly roughing it."

"Is that what you expected?"

"Honestly, Logan, I don't really know *what* I expected. I'm still a little shocked that this is my life for the next three months. I'm nervous and excited. I don't want to let you or the band down."

"Impossible. I knew nothing about this life when they hired me. It's not hard, just a lot of detail and organization. You have that in spades. Besides, it's not just you. It's both of us. We're a team."

"Let's get this party started," Cole says, climbing onto the bus, the rest of the band trailing on behind him. He slides in next to me, Kacen next to Logan, Gavin sits next to Kacen, and Tristan next to Cole. Logan and I are surrounded by musical hotness.

"Now what?" Logan asks.

"Now, we wait. Our first stop is Atlanta, which is about a four-hour drive," Kacen explains.

"That's a short jag compared to some of them. There will be nights that, as soon as the show is over, we pile on the bus and drive all night and some of the next day to get to the next show," Tristan adds.

"So, what do you do?" Logan asks.

"Play cards, but most of the time we sleep. It's exhausting at best. We write music, play Xbox. I'm not going to lie; it gets old fast, but with you here, I can see it being a hell of a lot more fun." Kacen wags his eyebrows.

"Who's up for a little gaming?" Gavin asks.

"You ready for me to kick your ass again so soon? I just demolished you yesterday," Tristan goads him.

"Bring it, fucker," Gavin fires back. They both move to the small couch that has a large flat-screen hanging on the wall across from it.

"Have you seen our room?" Kacen asks Logan.

She shakes her head, and that's all the answer he needs as he stands and pulls her with him. "Come on, I'll show you."

I watch as they walk to the back of the bus and disappear.

"Have you seen where you'll be sleeping?" Cole asks.

"No, we didn't make it past this point."

"Follow me." He stands and holds his hand out for me. I don't accept it as I stand on my own and follow him in the direction our friends just disappeared.

"This is it." He opens a door to a room that has four bunks. "The couch and the table also turn into beds, so if you ever want a change of scenery, that's an option as well," he explains.

"Which one is mine?" The space is not as small as I was expecting. Each one has a small TV that flips down from the top and what I assume are Bluetooth speakers in the corners. Thick curtains block out the rest of the room, giving a semblance of privacy.

"You can choose whichever one you want."

I survey the bunks. "Which one is yours?"

He shrugs. "We haven't picked yet."

I think about it and know immediately that I need to be on the bottom bunk. They all have a lot of height on me, so it will be easier for one of them to climb into the top. "I guess I'll take this one." I point to the bottom right.

He nods then goes to the door and opens it. "Stacy and I have claimed the right side, so you all can duke it out for the left," he yells to Gavin and Tristan.

"You picked the right too?"

He steps close, tucking my hair behind my ear. "Yeah, it puts me closer to you."

I expect a come on, a wink or even a smirk. I get none of the three. Just Cole surprising me again.

"So, what now?" I ask, stepping around him. I need the distance.

"Hmmm, how are you are cards? Rummy?"

"It's been a while, but I'm game." He nods and starts to reach for my hand. He must change his mind as he quickly drops his hands to his sides and stalks back to the living area. I follow behind him. He reaches up into a cabinet over the table and grabs a deck of cards and a notebook.

"Play to five hundred?" he asks.

"Isn't the name of the game five hundred rummy?" I question him.

"Yes, smartass." He taps the end of my nose with his index finger. "We often play longer. These road trips are brutal, and sometimes five hundred just isn't enough."

"Gotcha. Yeah, I think five hundred works for now." I slide into the booth and wait for him to deal the cards.

"So, why teaching?" His question takes me by surprise.

"I've always loved kids and school came easy to me. I had a few teachers who made it fun. That's important, and I thought I could be that person."

"So, why the pharmaceutical company?"

"It's hard to find a full-time teaching job. Most settle into a position and stay there until they retire. Unfortunately, with tight budgets, classrooms are filled over capacity and teachers can't give their students the attention they need."

"So, what happened with the pharmaceutical company? I remember Logan saying you were unhappy with it."

"Nothing specific, really. They talked a good game, had me convinced that I would be helping to educate physicians and nurses about the vaccines."

"Is that not what you were doing?"

"Yes and no. What they don't tell you is how busy the office staff and physicians are. It's hard to get even a few minutes of their time to listen to what you have to say. Not to mention here I am, an education major, telling a physician what treatment to recommend for their patients. They didn't treat me bad, but you could tell they were just listening because they had to when we would bring lunch or provide them with samples."

He nods. "I can see that. They're saving lives and all that shit."

I laugh at his comment. "Yeah, so I always felt as though I was a thorn in their side. It's just uncomfortable and not teaching at all, really. I have no clinical background, but that didn't matter; education major and nurses are who they hire. My team leader was a nurse, and she would travel with me to my sites once a month. It just . . . wasn't for me," I confess.

I watch as Cole concentrates on the cards in his hands before he lays out a spread and discards. "What about you?" I ask. "Has it always been music for you?"

"Yeah, I mean, I've always loved it. I started playing the guitar when I was ten. My grandparents bought me my own for birthday. The first time I played I was hooked."

"Did you ever think about what you'll do when this,"—I sweep my hand around the bus—"stops. When you all decide to stop?"

"Of course I've thought about it. The guys, we've talked about it. We've thrown around ideas such as starting our own label." He shrugs. "Who knows? I know the four of us have always been smart with our money and invested wisely. We could stop playing, touring, stop it all tomorrow and still be set for life."

Not able to make a play, I discard. "That's good, but what would you do?"

He seems to think about my question. "I don't know. I guess it just depends on if we start a label or what direction we go in. I'd like to think that I would find a place in the music world, but I don't know. I've never been much of a planner, really. Investing our royalties is the most planning I've ever done. I live each moment to the fullest."

"I didn't have a backup plan either. I'm a twenty-three-year-old college graduate who lives with her parents."

"Just recently. You lost your roommate, that's understandable." He's quick to defend me.

"Doesn't make it any easier. I was in a job I hated with no prospects of positions to use my education."

"It's all good, though." He stops what he's doing and grins. A grin that brings out his dimple, which I just discovered, and lights up his big brown eyes. "Now you're here with us. You're one of us. We're your backup plan."

"Yeah, I guess you are." I find myself grinning at him too.

CHAPTER 21

I GIVE MYSELF A MENTAL fist bump—I kept my cock in line and didn't make a pass at her all afternoon. Well, there was a minute when I was showing her the bunks that I had to touch her. I couldn't have controlled it even if I tried.

We arrived in Atlanta a few hours ago. We were all starving, so we made that our first order of business. Now, it's time to decide what we're doing for the night. The boys and I usually go out, but I can tell Kacen won't be.

"So, what's the plan?" he asks.

I look around at my brothers and no one jumps at throwing out suggestions. "I think I'm just going to chill here," Tristan says, looking at his phone. Something is going on with him. I wonder if he's met someone. He's been glued to that phone the past few months.

"I'm not really feeling it either," Gavin chimes in.

I stare at both of them, trying to figure out what I'm missing. Something's up.

Although, once my eyes land on Stacy, I can't seem to find the desire to go out either.

"Cole," Kacen says.

"I'm good," I reply. *I would rather stay in and talk to your wife's best friend than get my dick wet with a random.*

Fuck!

What is she doing to me? This is a first. It goes unsaid, but I know they're all thinking it. Never have all three of us passed up a night out, especially at the beginning of a tour when we're fresh. A night here or there, sure, but never all three of us.

"Ladies?" Kacen asks.

"I'm exhausted," Logan tells him.

"I'm good with staying in as well. What's in store for tomorrow?" Stacy asks.

"Interviews with the local radio station in the morning, sound check in the afternoon and then the show starts at eight," Logan rattles off our schedule.

"Sounds like you all have an early morning anyway," Stacy says.

"Right, well, we'll see you in the morning." Kacen, who is standing behind Logan, places his hands on her hips and guides her toward the bedroom.

"I'm going to watch a movie." Gavin retreats to his bunk.

"Sleep," Tristan mumbles, following along behind them.

Once again, it's just the two of us. "What about you, sweets?"

Stacy sits on the couch. "I'm not tired yet. I think I'll just read for a little while."

I watch as she reaches into her bag and pulls out her Kindle. "Do you care if I watch TV? Will it bother you? I'm not ready for the bunk just yet." It's not a complete stretch of the truth. I'm not ready to leave her, and that's something that is alarming, but not enough that I ignore the desire to spend more time with her. I like getting to know her, which is a new concept for me.

"Nope. When I'm reading, I can block everything else out." She settles into the corner of the couch. I reach into the storage cabinet above her and pull out a throw blanket, unfold it, and drape it over her. The smile she gives me makes my heart race. She's fucking beautiful.

"Thank you, Cole." Her voice is soft.

I can't speak, not without begging her to let me inside, so instead, I nod and sit beside her.

I scroll through the channels until I finally settle on the movie *Speed*. It's older, but it's a good one. And it stars Sandra Bullock which is a bonus.

I glue my eyes to the TV—at least, I try. I steal glances at Stacy and she's oblivious, so engrossed in whatever it is she's reading. I watch as she bites her lip and, a few pages later, a small smile graces her lip. She's fully captivated by the world that author has created.

I try to focus on the movie, and it works for about twenty minutes or so, until I hear sniffles. Whipping my head around to look at her, I see tears flowing down her cheeks. Without thinking, I reach out and link my fingers through hers. This gets her attention.

A watery smile greets me as she chuckles through her tears. "Not a word, Hampton," she warns me.

Refusing to let go of her hand, I turn to face her. My other hand cups her cheek and I wipe away her tears with my thumb. It's fucking irrational as hell, but I hate seeing her cry. It's the story, I get it, but that doesn't mean I like it.

"I don't like seeing you cry," I admit.

She chuckles again as more tears fall from her eyes. "I can't seem to help it. Some of these books, just . . . gut me. I love it, though."

The tears cause her green eyes to sparkle. "You're beautiful." She blushes. This girl . . . she's not like anyone I've ever met.

"How's your movie?" She pulls her hand from mine and wipes at her cheeks.

I leave my hand where it falls, on her thigh. "I've seen it before," I tell her.

She glances up at the TV. "Yeah, this is an oldie but goodie."

That smile.

"Are you finished with your book?"

She nods. "Yeah, another happily ever after."

"With tears?"

"With tears," she agrees. "It's the way he loves her." She blushes at her admission.

"Feel like watching the rest of this with me?" I try to keep from sounding too hopeful. She could sit there and read all damn night for all

I care. I just want her to be next to me.

I'm freaked the fuck out, because that is not something I have ever thought about anyone. I don't like chics to just hang around, and I certainly don't long to just be in their presence.

These next three months are going to be interesting if this is how it's going to go.

"I don't want to cramp your style," she teases.

I settle back against the couch and raise my arm, inviting her to lie against my chest. It's only been a couple of times that I've done this, all with her, and I crave it.

She places her Kindle back in her bag on the floor and settles against me. I reach down and pull the blanket up over her. Once she's comfortable, I flick off the lights. We're now cast in just the glow from the television screen.

Her breathing eventually evens out; peering down, I see that she's asleep. I hold her a little tighter and close my eyes. My last thought is that a man could get used to this.

CHAPTER 22

"SHH!" I HEAR LOGAN HISS.

I slowly open my eyes and blink away the sleep. *Shit! We fell asleep last night.* I squeeze my eyes closed, wishing Logan and whoever it is she's hissing at would be quiet so I would have slept a little longer. To make matters worse, Cole is starting to wake up, and he's drawing circles on my lower back. I want to yell at them to go back to bed so I can enjoy this rare moment of sweet Cole. Instead, I try to move his hand, but he's not having it.

"Stop, baby," he mumbles.

Shit. Shit. Shit.

"Baby?" Kacen says, loud enough that we're both opening our eyes.

I quickly sit up, as does Cole. He blinks a few times and roughly runs his hands over his face.

"What the hell is going on here?" Kacen demands.

"Babe, calm down," Logan tries to soothe him.

"Fucking hell, Kace. We fell asleep watching a movie," Cole bites back.

"You called her 'baby,'" he retorts.

Cole shrugs. "And your point is? I was fucking comfortable."

"I fucking told you, Cole."

"Chill the fuck out, man. I know I heard you the tenth fucking time you lectured me. We fell asleep, end of story." Cole stands and makes his way to the bathroom.

"Kacen." My voice is low. "He's telling you the truth. I read for a little while and then we watched the rest of *Speed*. We fell asleep." I hate that he's so angry about this. I'm beginning to wonder if I made the wrong decision.

"You all 'just fell asleep' at the house too," he says, with less anger in his voice.

"Kacen Michael, you need to stay out of it. Who cares if they fell asleep? Who cares if they slept together? They are both adults and can make their own decisions. Who are you to tell them what they can and cannot do?" Logan lays into him.

"She's your best friend."

"And he's yours. They are also two consenting adults who do not want or need your permission to do whatever the hell it is they want to do."

"I don't want it to cause problems." His voice is softer now that he's talking to his wife.

"*You're* going to, acting the way you are. Stay out of it."

Cole comes back into the room and sits on the couch beside me. "It's not a secret that I want her. Nothing you say can keep that from happening."

WOW!

"She's not a groupie," Kacen says through his teeth.

"You think I don't know that?"

"Stop! Nothing happened. We fell asleep. Kacen, I appreciate your concern, but regardless of what, if anything, happens between Cole and me, or hell, me and Gavin or Tristan . . ." I pause when Cole growls beside me. "It will not be any of your concern. I promise you that it will not change my relationship with Logan, and it would take more than a one-night stand to keep me from this amazing opportunity you've given me."

Tristan and Gavin must have heard the commotion as they are now both awake and sitting at the table. Of course, they arrived just in time to hear my little tirade.

"Stacy, you tell me when and where." Tristan winks at me.

"Ditto." Gavin grins cheekily.

"Fuck you both," Cole seethes. "Hands off."

"I'm flattered," I tell them. "But it's not happening. With any of you." I make a point to look at all three of them. Gavin and Tristan are wearing matching sleepy grins. Cole looks . . . sad, with a mix of anger evident. I don't even take the time to figure out what that means.

"Right, you all have to be at the radio station in an hour. It's a fifteen-minute commute, so get moving. Breakfast casserole is on the stove," Logan says.

And just like that, the discussion is over. The four of them grumble their thanks and love of Logan's cooking while filling their plates. She takes a seat next to me on the couch and pats my leg.

"Sorry about all of that," she whispers.

I shake my head, letting her know she doesn't need to apologize.

"So, did you finish that book?" she asks.

"Yes, it was so good."

"Did you cry?"

"Like a baby." I grin. I love that we have the same taste in books.

"I was worried at first," Cole says between bites from his seat at the table.

From the look on her face, Logan is thrilled that Cole seemed to care.

"What is it you call it, babe? 'Ugly girl cry'?" Kacen winks at her.

"Yes, and I'm not ashamed," Logan says, head held high.

"Most of the time, they break you, but put you back together again," I tell him.

"I don't like to see my wife cry," Kacen grumbles.

I chance a look at Cole to find him already looking at me. Something passes between us, Kacen's words almost exactly what he said to me last night. This unspoken connection confuses me. It's nothing I would have expected from Cole.

Logan clears her throat, pulling my attention away from Cole.

Busted.

She winks at me. Logan doesn't miss a thing.

"Later," I mouth to her. I know my best friend, and she's going to want details.

"You sure you don't want to come with us?" Kacen asks for the third time in the last half hour.

"I'm sure. Stacy and I are going to go over the rest of today's schedule." He finally agrees, kisses her, and the guys are off.

"Dish!" Logan says as soon as the bus door closes.

I laugh at her giddiness for the scoop. "Not much to dish. He wants to sleep with me, and I keep telling him no."

"That's it?" She sounds sad.

"In a nutshell. We hung out before I made my decision to accept the job, which you know. Then yesterday and last night, we hung out pretty much most of the time."

"Kacen said it's not like the three of them to not want to go out. Usually, they're out strolling for female companions."

"Yeah, not sure what's up with that. Tristan and Gavin both seem to be preoccupied with their phones lately."

"I know Gavin is spending more time with the label, learning the ropes and whatnot. They're thinking of opening their own label someday."

I nod. "Cole mentioned that."

"I guess they've been talking about it more recently. Kacen is afraid that once the baby gets here, I won't want to travel with him. I told him we might need our own bus, but it's possible. I wouldn't want to do a year-long tour, but a few months at a time with a break might not be that bad of an idea."

"I'm sure it won't be easy, but if anyone can do it, it's the two of you."

Logan smiles. "So, admit it, it's killing you to keep telling him no."

Leave it to my bestie to get straight to the point. "I might have maybe had a fantasy or two," I admit sheepishly.

"I knew it! It's the hair, right?"

"It *is* nice to hold onto when he's kissing me." *Shit!*

"What? When? Why the hell am I just now finding out about this?"

Ugh! Me and my big mouth. I spend the next twenty minutes giving her the basics of what's been going on with us the past several months.

"He's different with you," she tells me once I've given her an edited version. Some things I just want for me.

"He's chasing me. He's realized he has to change his game. He knows I'm not going to fall for his regular bullshit. The 'It'll be good between us' cheesy-ass lines."

Logan throws her head back in laughter. "True, but it's more than that. I just have this feeling."

"It's the pregnancy hormones."

For some reason, we both find this funny. My theory is that it's because she is deliriously happy and living life with the man she loves, starting a family. Laughter is happiness.

CHAPTER 23

THE RADIO INTERVIEW LASTED FOUR hours. There was a last-minute change, so we were on the early morning show and then the four of us recorded a Hot Thirty weekend countdown. This was sprung on us when we got there. Apparently, Brian Wilson, who is our label CEO, said it would be no big deal. He's always doing stupid shit like that. If it weren't for Jones, we would have left a long time ago; he's a kick-ass manager, even though his boss is a dick.

We had to go straight from the station to sound check, so we grabbed a quick bite to eat in the dressing room and then spent the last three hours doing sound check. The four of us are kind of perfectionists; we want to make sure our fans get their money's worth every show.

I haven't seen Stacy since this morning, and I have no idea if she's pissed off at me for what happened. It's still hard for me to wrap my head around the fact that I actually care if she is. Another first.

"Where the hell are they?" Kacen paces back and forth in our dressing room. We take the stage in twenty minutes, and the girls are still not here. Kacen sent two of the appointed bodyguards to the bus to escort them here.

"It's been what, ten minutes?" Tristan asks.

The door opens and the ladies in question walk in smiling and laughing. Stacy is wearing black jeans that look like she was poured into them and high-heeled boots. Her silver sweater shimmers in the light. Her hair is pulled to the side, exposing her slender neck.

I shove my hands in my pockets to keep from reaching out for her. She stands just inside the door, looking unsure.

"Look at you." Gavin leans in and kisses her cheek. "Ready for the action?"

"This your first time being behind the scenes at a concert?" Tristan asks, giving her a one-armed hug.

I hate that their hands are on her.

"It is." Her emerald eyes light up. "I'm excited."

"It's a rush." Gavin grins.

"I want the two of you to stay together. There will be a guard with you, and you'll be sitting stage-side," Kacen explains.

Excitement runs through me. I love the thrill of the crowd, the lights, the screaming fans. It's a rush, and I'm excited for both of them to get to see it firsthand. See that yes, we may be a group of goofy guys, but we take music seriously. We are damn fine musicians, if I do say so myself.

"Got it," they reply in unison. Then they break out in laughter, and if I didn't know better, I would think they were both a little tipsy.

"Knock, knock." Jones slowly opens our door. "You ready to rock?" He's asked us this before every show since the first.

"Always," the four us respond. This causes the girls to giggle again. I admit it's rather infectious, their excitement.

"You're on in five." He leaves, Cassidy trailing behind him.

"I'll meet up with you," Gavin says as he runs after them.

Tristan opens the door, and the rest of us pile out. Kacen and Logan are huddled close together; I know he's doing it to keep the press from hounding her.

Reaching out, I pull Stacy to my side. "Stay close. Those fuckers are vultures." I motion with my head to the swarm of press we have to pass in order to get backstage. We all hate it, but it's a necessary evil in this business.

Stacy doesn't hesitate as she wraps her arm around my waist and buries her head in my chest. This makes me grin—me, the guy who's always avoided this type of situation, grins at the idea that I can protect her from them. Any other girl and I would let her fend for herself. Not Stacy.

We make it through the crowd and lead the girls to their seats, side-stage. She's still in my arms, even though there's no longer a need, not here on stage. Leaning down, I place my lips next to her ear. "How about a kiss for luck?"

She surprises me when she says, "You really think you need it?"

I chuckle as I nuzzle her neck. "The luck? No, we got this. To taste your lips? Most definitely."

"Cole." She breathes my name and it's sexy as fuck.

I'm playing with fire, knowing Kace and Logan are standing beside us, but I can't seem to find any fucks to give right now. I turn her so we're facing each other, my arms wrapped around her. She looks over at our friends, and I take a step back behind the thick black curtain, out of their line of sight. I don't wait for her to give me permission, just place my lips against hers. I take my time tasting her, enjoying the feel of her in my arms.

This is another new experience for me. I never bring girls behind the scenes to watch the show—none of us do. It's always after-show hookups, kind of like an unwritten rule or something.

I slow the kiss, hating that it has to end. She looks up at me with those emerald eyes of hers, full of lust and . . . happiness. Standing on tiptoes, she whispers in my ear, "Good luck, Cole."

And just like that, she's on the other side of the curtain, leaving me dazed and captivated—completely fucking captivated—by her charm.

Taking a deep breath, I get my shit together and walk around the curtain. Kacen and the guys are already on stage. I walk past Stacy and smack her on the ass, then keep walking as though nothing happened. No one saw the kiss, but all the fucking roadies saw that; all eyes are glued on the two beautiful women, and they need to know she's off-limits.

Fuck! I need to get my head in the game. It's a packed crowd tonight, and we always deliver 110 percent.

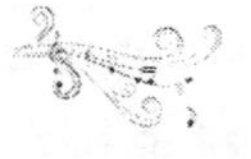

We killed it! That's all I can say. The crowd was energetic and the entire show fucking rocked. Stacy seemed to be having a great time as well, and I admit it was nice to be able to turn my head and see her. The two of them never moved once from the spots side-stage. Every time I looked over—which, I admit, was more often than I should have—they were dancing and singing along.

Kacen bids the crowd a final good night and the lights go down. Even in the darkness, I head straight toward her, needing to taste those lips again. I couldn't give a fuck who sees me do it.

As I make my way over, I hear both of them cheering. My pulse quickens. It's a fucking rush like no other to know she enjoyed the show—not just because she wants my cock, but because she really enjoyed it.

"EEEKKK!" is all I hear as her body slams into mine. I catch her as she jumps into my arms. "That was amazing! You guys killed it."

Her face is lit up, her hair wild from dancing, her emerald eyes shimmering with excitement. I tighten my hold on her ass, and her legs squeeze tight around my waist. Satisfied that she's not going to fall, I kiss her. No, I fucking *devour* her.

My tongue slips past her lips and she immediately opens for me. I kiss her like my life depends on it. She moans and it fuels me as I squeeze her ass tighter and rub her against my hard cock. This girl, that's what she does to me. Just saying her name has my cock standing at attention.

Much to my disappointment, she pulls away, her lips swollen from mine. Slowly, she releases the grip her legs have on my waist and slides down my body, taking a step back. I'm reaching for her when Tristan picks her up and spins her around. He places a chaste kiss on her lips and sets her back on her feet.

"What did you think?" he asks.

I reach out and grab her hand, pulling her to my side; thankfully, she doesn't protest. Not fond of punching one of my best friends, a guy I claim as my brother, but that kiss. . . . Yeah, I could punch his ass right now.

"You guys rocked," she happily praises him.

"They did, didn't they?" Logan says as she and Kacen join us.

"It's a fucking rush," Gavin chimes in.

I fight the urge to tell them all to fuck off so I can disappear with her.

She pulls out of my hold, which pisses me off because she's now hugging Gavin, then Kacen. I get it; she's congratulating them, but dammit, she just had her tight little body wrapped around mine.

I miss her heat.

How fucked up is that? I'm losing my fucking mind over this girl.

"Now what?" she asks.

"Now, we shower," Gavin says, throwing his arm over her shoulder. I watch as he rubs his wet hair against her cheek.

I take a step toward them when Tristan's arm lands on my stomach, holding me back.

"Tonight, we're done. Some nights, we have meet-and-greets after the show, even radio or television interviews. Tonight, however, we're done," Kacen explains.

Stacy makes eye contact with me. Once she has my attention, she makes a show of lifting Gavin's arm from her shoulder and stepping next to Logan. I relax, as does Tristan.

"Are you all hungry? I can call and have food delivered to the bus. They do that type of thing, right?" she asks.

"Yes, just tell them who it's for and they'll deliver. I'm thinking hoagies," Logan says.

"Great. Why don't we head back to the bus and order the food while these sweaty beasts get showered?" Stacy catches my eye again. "Any special requests?"

You. "We'll eat anything, sweets. Just make sure there's a lot of it," I answer.

Kacen motions for the bodyguard to come join us. "Make sure the girls get back to the bus. Can you stay outside until we get there?"

"Yes, sir," he immediately responds. He talks into his wrist and two more guys appear.

I watch them walk away, not willing to take my eyes off her.

"What the fuck was that?" Tristan asks.

I meet his stare head-on, but say nothing.

"Explain," Tristan growls. "You were ready to throw down with Gav. It was harmless, man."

I rub my hands over my face. "I don't fucking know, all right?"

"You don't know? You don't fucking know? Really, Cole? You were ready to punch his ass!" he yells.

"He was touching her!" I yell back.

The three of them stop, mouths hanging open.

Fuck me.

"She got to you." Kacen is suddenly grinning.

"No. Yes. Hell, I don't know. This is new territory for me. I'm not the jealous type, but I wanted to punch all three of you for touching her." I punch Tristan in the arm. "You fucking kissed her."

He rubs his arm. "Damn, it was just a peck, fucker."

"Keep your lips away from her, and your dick." I turn to face Gavin. "That goes for you too."

"Kace told you not to fuck her," Tristan chimes in.

Shit. They are *never* going to let me live this down. I now regret giving Kacen a hard time about Logan.

"I didn't fuck her," I mumble.

"I'm sorry, what? I couldn't hear you. It sounded like you said you didn't fuck her." Gavin smirks.

"You heard me. I didn't fuck her."

"Holy shit," Tristan whispers.

Kacen throws his arm over my shoulders. "Welcome to the bright side, my man."

I turn to look at him. "The bright side?"

He nods. "Yeah, trust me. There's a lot to be said for being with only one woman."

"Who said I was only going to be with one woman?"

All three of them throw their heads back in laughter. "Come on, the girls are waiting on us," Kacen says, dropping his arm and walking off.

We follow behind him, my mind reeling. The jealousy, the way I think of nothing but her, the fact that I can just hang out with her, no sex, and be perfectly content.

What the hell does it all mean?

CHAPTER 24

I MADE IT THROUGH MY fist week. The shows are selling out, and the guys are constantly hyped on adrenaline. Cole assures me that by the end of the tour, their enthusiasm wanes in comparison to what it is now.

Cole.

He and I have been spending a lot of time together. We hang out with the others, but when they go their separate ways, we usually end up hanging out. I tell him he can go out, but he never does. In fact, it's been a week and I'm starting to feel like I'm getting cheated from having the full tour experience.

I expected wild parties and sex—you know, everything you imagine when you think rock tour. The only thing I wasn't expecting was drugs, since I know all four of them are anti-drug. Again, unusual, but I'm starting to see that Soul Serenade is nothing if not unique in their own right.

Today is a rare day off, as the next show is the day after next, and it's only about a six-hour drive from here. I know the others all have plans for the day. I really have nothing going on, and there's nothing I want to do really. It's good to have a day to just relax.

The bus is quiet. Tristan and Cole are still sleeping, and Gavin left earlier claiming to have business with the label. The newlyweds left about a half hour ago to do some shopping. Kacen apparently loved the idea of buying the baby something in every city.

"Hey, Stace," Tristan says groggily.

"Afternoon, sleepyhead."

He grins. "I need my beauty sleep."

I chuckle. "I think you're good, Tristan."

"Should I be worried?" Cole's sleepy voice startles me.

"Worried?" Tristan asks, confused.

"My girl just told you you're beautiful," Cole deadpans.

I focus my attention back to my Kindle.

Tristan spits the drink of milk he just took. "Uh . . . we were just kidding around. Your girl?" he questions.

I pretend to be reading. I'm not. I tap the screen and bring up a book I've already read; that way, I can tap the pages and not lose my spot. I don't want them to know that I'm hanging on every word.

"Not yet," Cole tells him. "I'm working on it, though."

There is not one hint of teasing in his tone. I'm too big of a chicken to look at him, to see if the expression on his face tells a different story.

"All right then. I'm supposed to meet Gavin at the sports bar down the street for some pool. You all want to come with?"

"No," Cole says.

"Stacy?" Tristan calls my name.

I look up, acting as though I wasn't listening. "I'm sorry, what?"

"Gav and I are going to play some pool at a place just down the road. You want to come with us?"

I don't look at Cole, but I can feel his eyes bore into me. "No, but thanks, though. I think I'm just going to enjoy the quiet while I can."

"All right, well, if you change your mind, just call me and we'll send one of the guys back to get you."

"I'm good, but thanks. Have fun and be safe." Logan's mothering tendencies have rubbed off on me when it comes to this lovable group of rockers.

"Have you eaten?" Cole asks once Tristan's gone.

"Not since breakfast."

"Let me take a shower, and then we can go grab something to eat." He leans in, kisses me on the forehead, then stands and heads toward the bathroom.

He's been like this for the last week. He hasn't given me his usual "we would be good together. One night is all we need" speech in a few weeks, and I've been feeling this gradual shift between us. I've come to see a different side of him, but does a tiger really change his stripes? This could be his way to get what he wants, which is apparently me underneath him.

He's showered and ready to go in record time.

"Where are we going?" I ask.

"I don't know. I thought we could take a walk and see what catches our attention."

I watch as he slips a hair tie on his wrist and grabs his sunglasses. I've watched them all make some type of effort to be incognito when they go out in public.

He holds his hand out for me and I easily slip my fingers between his. He's been this sweet, sexy guy all week, but I'm waiting for the "when can we fuck" or something to that effect to fall from his lips.

We walk through the city, and the silence between us is comfortable; we're simply just two people holding hands, enjoying the slow pace of the day.

"How about there?" He points to a food truck.

"This will be a first for me," I admit.

"Really? It's kind of like fair food, without the rides." He winks.

We both order a cheeseburger and a large fries to split. It smells amazing. Cole leads us over to a picnic table that sits next to the truck.

"They leave picnic tables in the street?"

He chuckles, pointing to the food truck. "They bring it. I can only assume that it helps business. The truck is convenient, but walking and eating is not always as easy."

"Makes sense."

"So, how are you liking being on the road so far?" he asks once we're seated.

I place the fries on a part of my cheeseburger wrapper between us. Cole works on opening a few ketchup packets. "It's not what I expected—at least, not yet."

"Not yet?"

"It's just that I expected more . . . parties and groupies and just . . . you know, all the stuff you hear and think of when you think rock tour."

"Disappointed?" He smirks.

"No, I'm not disappointed," I say, with a little more sass than necessary. "It's just not what I expected."

"Do you regret it? Your decision to come with us?"

By the tone of his voice, it's almost as though he dreads hearing the answer. "Not at all. I mean, it's only been a week, but it's been fun to see it all behind the scenes. Not only that, but I get to work with my bestie."

He nods and takes a bite of his burger. I don't even think he chewed, because he's already talking again—with no food in his mouth, I might add.

"You forgot to mention the best damn rock group who just so happens to have a sexy lead guitarist." He winks and shoves the rest of his burger in his mouth.

"How could I forget about Gavin? He's every girl's wet dream," I quip. I'm just messing with him; I know Gavin is bass guitar and Cole is lead, but he can't be the one having all the fun.

"Are you fucking kidding me right now?" he asks. He's dead serious, and I see that my joke is not as funny to him.

I quickly snatch a fry out of the container and throw it at him. "Yes, Mr. Hampton, I'm fucking kidding you."

He easily catches the fry and pops it into his mouth. I watch as he chews once and swallows before he narrows his gaze on me. "Not funny, sweets."

"Oh, come on. You have to admit I got you."

"You can have me any way you want me, Stacy."

Serious. That's the first word that comes to my head. The look in his eyes tells me this statement is different from all the others. At least that's how it feels.

"Hmmm, let's see," I start, tapping my index finger on my chin. "I think I want you . . . to be sweet Cole." I immediately feel my face heat once the words slip past my lips.

"Sweet Cole?"

I take a drink of my water to stall. *Why can I not just keep my damn mouth shut? Oh, well. Too late now.* "Yeah." I re-cap my water. "You know, the guy you've been the last couple of weeks. You're nice to me, and you've toned down the 'we will fuck' attitude. It's been good." I shrug. "I like getting to know this side of you." I might as well lay it all out there, since I've already shoved my foot in my mouth.

CHAPTER 25

SWEET COLE.

Fuck me, that's the first time a woman other than my sister or mom has ever referred to me as 'sweet." Well, Logan, but she's just like my sister.

Sweet Cole. I let those words bounce around in my head.

I don't know what exactly she constitutes as "sweet." It's not like I've been all romantic and shit with her. I'm just being me—well, me when I'm thinking about something other than sliding between her thighs. It's been . . . fun, much to my surprise. This hanging out and getting to know someone isn't as bad as I would have thought.

"Sweet?" I finally ask.

"Yeah, you're not all 'I can't wait to feel you' and all that other game you have going on."

"Game?" I laugh.

"Yes, game. You're a player, Cole. It's kind of like a game of Monopoly. You roll the dice and land on a property. You take full advantage, but you're itching for your next turn, to roll the dice again and see where you land."

Monopoly? "I don't play games, Stacy. Yes, I've slept with a lot of women, but I never lead them on. I never go into the night with them thinking it's going to be more than what it is—just fucking. That's it. If they romanticize that they can change me, that's on them. I'm always open and up-front with them."

"I believe you. You've always been honest that you want to sleep with me, I get that. But these last few weeks, you've toned that down." I watch as she averts her gaze before continuing. "I just figured that you had lost interest."

Lost interest? Has she lost her damn mind? Reaching out, I caress her cheek. "Definitely still interested." I trace her lips with my thumb.

I watch as she closes her eyes and relaxes into my touch. She wants me too. It's written all over her face.

Finally, she opens her eyes, and I can see the war waging in them. She feels this connection too, but she's fighting it. I know she said she wants more. If she would just give this a chance, it would be a night that I can guarantee neither one of us would ever forget.

Leaning back, she breaks contact. "What's next?"

I stand to gather our trash. "I thought we could just walk around and see if anything interests us."

She nods and stands from her seat. I quickly throw away our trash and reach for her hand. Surprisingly, she doesn't pull away. I'll take every damn chance I can to get my hands on her.

"So, no longer a food truck virgin," I say, trying to get that easy banter back between us. I peek over at her and she's blushing. That's sexy as fuck.

"It was good. I don't know why I was skeptical."

Pulling our combined hands to my lips, I kiss her knuckles. "I'll never steer you wrong, sweets." Letting our hands fall back between us, I survey the area, looking for something for us to get into. That's when I see it.

"Stacy, you ever ridden go-karts?"

She grins. "Yeah, but it's been years."

Her grin is infectious, and I suddenly feel like a damn teenager. I lead us to the storefront and purchase two all-day passes.

"All day?" she asks.

"Yeah, you can't ride just once, and standing in line each time for a ticket just wastes time."

"What if we only ride twice?"

I give her the "you know better than that" look.

She grins.

"Now, which ones do you want to ride first?"

"The fastest."

Her answer surprises me. "Really?"

"Uh, yeah. I'm about to kick your ass, Hampton."

This girl.

"You think so?" I try to hide my grin, I really do, but it's impossible when I see hers shining back at me.

"Oh, yeah, I got this." She hip-checks me and takes off toward the line.

I stand frozen for a few minutes, just watching her. I can't ever remember having a better time with a woman. I would rather have lunch with her and that smile than sex with a random any day.

WHOA! What the fuck am I thinking? I shake off the thought and search for her in the crowd. I spot her standing at the gate, underneath a sign claiming that particular track is the fastest in the complex. Her hands are on her hips and she's tapping her foot, watching me.

Waiting for me.

There is something, a feeling deep in the pit of my gut that I've never felt before. My feet move toward her; suddenly, nothing matters but being next to her. When I reach her, I snake an arm around her waist and pull her in to my chest, kissing the top of her head. She hesitates for a few seconds before sliding her arms around my waist.

She let's me hold her.

Something I've never wanted to do.

Unexpectedly, it's *all* I want to do.

With her.

Only her.

She pulls away and I fight the urge to groan in protest. Looking up at me with those big green eyes, I don't know if she's about to ask questions, or if she's just trying to figure out what the hell is happening, but I don't give her time to do either. Instead, I lean down and place a soft, tender kiss on her lips.

That's another first for me. There was never a reason to show tenderness or emotion. Hell, with half the women I've been with, my lips didn't get close to them.

I slide my fingers between hers and lead us to the line. Taking our places, I lean against the fence and pull her back into my arms. This time, it has nothing to do with convincing her to spend the night in my bed and everything to do with her.

Just her.

CHAPTER 26

ANOTHER SHIFT. NOT SURE WHAT it is, but everything is once again . . . different. He's holding me in his arms like I'm his. I know I should protest, pull away, but the feeling is like none other, so I'm going to roll with it. Give myself today to bask in the illusion that this is real. That he doesn't want anyone but me.

It's wrong on so many levels. I've never been one who can detach my feelings, but I will deal with the consequences. In this moment, I feel . . . cherished.

As we move up in the line, his hands never leave me. He's either holding my hand, my hips, or his arm is slung over my shoulder.

And the kisses . . . he's taking sweet Cole to a whole new level with the attention he's raining down on me today.

A girl could get used to this.

"You ready, sweets?" he asks, lips next to my ear.

Peering up at him, he's wearing a smile that seems to light up his face more often than not these past few weeks. "The question is, are you ready to get beat by a girl?" I fire back.

He throws his head back and laughs before releasing his hold on me to pull a hair tie from his wrist. I watch as he gathers his long locks and wraps it all up in a messy bun. Let me be clear, Cole Hampton can rock a man-bun. It's not really been my thing up to this point. I've seen pictures all over my social media, and there are very few who capture my attention. Cole, though, he's got it. He rocks it, and I can guarantee there are panties dropping everywhere when he does.

Hair contained, his hands rest on my hips as he pulls me in to him. Leaning down, he replies, "Bring it, baby." His brown eyes are sparkling.

Lethal.

He turns me in his arms so I'm facing the track, and I see that it's finally our turn to race. I sprint toward the front cart, knowing I'll need every advantage I can get. It's been years since I've been on one of these things. I don't know where Cole is; I'm too focused on strapping myself in and getting comfortable in my seat. After the attendant checks my seat belt, I place my hands on the steering wheel, excitement coursing through me. I feel like a kid again.

Wheel gripped tight, my eyes stay glued to the light, one foot on the brake, the other poised over the throttle. I'm a woman on a mission.

Finally, the caution light pop's up and it's time to move. I race off the line and the attendant yells to "Slow down." I know he's yelling at me. I'm not supposed to dart out of the gate, but I'm excited and I really, *really* want to beat Cole. Bragging rights are a beautiful thing, especially when it's against a man's man like Cole. I can see him brooding over the loss already. The thought only fuels my excitement.

I drive as fast as I can without getting the stink eye and shaking fist from the attendant. I want to turn around and look for Cole, but I refuse to break my concentration.

As I come around the last corner, I see the green light and a teenage girl waving a plastic flag. Green means go.

Game on!

I punch the gas and hold on tight. The wind is whipping through my hair and laughter bubbles out of me. I take the next curve without lifting from the throttle and slide through the corner like I'm Danica Patrick. I can feel my face splitting with the grin I'm wearing. I'm having a blast, and it's for me. Not to beat Cole, although that would be a bonus; right now, I'm just enjoying the moment.

Our group of racers must be good because we don't have one caution. All fifteen laps, I keep the throttle matted to the floor and fly around corners, laughing and grinning like a fool. When the caution light comes on, I slow my kart and drive back into the lineup. I wait until we're given the all clear to unbuckle my seat belt and climb out. My feet barely hit the pavement before I feel his strong arms lift me up.

"Hell yeah! You killed it out there!" He squeezes me tight before placing me back on my feet.

"You got beat by a girl," I tease him.

I don't get the response I expected. "Sweets, I'm six-foot-four and weigh 180 pounds. What are you, five-six and a buck ten? Your cart was lighter than mine," he tries to rationalize my win. "Besides, I'm good with you beating me."

That's the part I didn't expect. "Oh, yeah? And why is that, Mr. Hampton?"

His hand on the small of my back, he leads us away from the karts and through the exit gate, away from the mass of people. He stops next to a pillar, turning so he's leaning against it. His hands wrap around my waist and he pulls me close.

I'm watching him, waiting for an answer. He tucks my crazy, windblown hair behind my ear, his eyes locked on mine. "You want to know why?" His voice is husky.

A nod is the only response I'm capable of.

He brings me closer, a feat I would have thought impossible, our bodies touching everywhere.

Soft vs. hard.

"I'm good with it because I get to take the winner home with me." He smirks.

I slap my hands against his chest as we both lose ourselves to the laughter of his statement.

"I might be going home with you, as you say, but you won't be reaping the rewards."

His smile is still there, but his eyes show a different emotion altogether. One I can't quite decipher. "The reward is being with you."

My mouth drops open.

He kisses me on the forehead and releases me. "Now, which one do you want to ride next?"

Just like that. No big deal that I'm swooning in the middle of a damn go-kart track thing—whatever this place is. No big deal that he just made my heart skip a beat, that my plan to steel my emotions just flew out the damn window. No big deal that he's chipping away at that wall I built, refusing myself intimacy with anyone who didn't want more. No big deal that those six words just got him what he's been after for months. It's in this moment that I realize it's always been inevitable. I'm going to let Cole Hampton give me what he assures will be the best night of my life. Then, I'm going to have to pick my heart up off the ground and act as though it's no big deal.

How does one come back from that?

We spend the next three hours racing from track to track, acting like teenagers.

"I'm done," I tell him. We just finished what feels like ride number fifty, and I'm exhausted and hungry.

"Hungry?" he asks.

It's like he can read my mind. "Yes."

"Starving," he replies with a boyish grin. Holding his hand out for me, I don't fight it, lacing my fingers through his. He leads us back to the sidewalk. "What sounds good?"

"Anything. I'm not a picky eater."

He nods and we walk about a block before he stops and points to a pizza place. I smile, letting him know it sounds good to me. We spend the next hour eating and talking about random things that mean nothing but in this moment feel like everything.

"I didn't think you were ever coming back," Logan says as soon as we walk onto the bus. Looking around, I see the four of them sitting around the table playing cards.

"Didn't know we needed to be."

"Well, we were getting worried. You've been gone a long time."

Kacen laughs. "Baby, we told you she was fine. She was with Cole."

Cole, who is standing behind me, gently runs his fingers up my spine. It's like he's trying to tell me that he agrees with Kacen.

"You should have just texted me."

"I did." She sighs. "You didn't answer your damn phone."

I reach around to retrieve my phone from my back pocket, but Cole beats me to it. He slides it out and gently lays it in my palm, his fingers trailing over mine. I try not to shudder at the contact. I bring my arm back around and tap the button and, sure enough, I have four missed calls from Logan. "Sorry, I didn't hear it. Or feel it. We were riding go-karts, so my ass was vibrating the entire time. Didn't know it was my phone," I explain.

"We called you too, man," Kacen says to Cole.

"Turned it off," his gruff voice pipes up from behind me.

"Why would you do that?" Logan questions him. The guys just look at him, all wearing smirks.

"Day off" is his half-ass reply.

"Well, now that everyone's here, can we eat? I'm starving," Gavin pleads.

"We just ate," Cole says.

"Well, that leaves us. You all ready to head out?" Tristan asks.

"You sure you don't want to come with?" Logan asks me.

"I'm worn out. We walked all over the city and road go-karts for hours. I'm ready to just relax. Besides, we roll out early in the morning, right?"

"Yeah," Kacen answers. "It's about a six-hour drive, so we'll probably head out around five or so. I doubt any of us will even be up."

"That's still hard to get used to."

"I agree. You wake up, look out the window and see highway. It's different for sure," Logan agrees. "Cole?"

He again runs his hands up my spine. They can't see what he's doing, and I have to fight against reacting. He's been touchy-feely all day, as have I, but it was just us. With them. . . .

"I'm beat. This one kicked my ass today."

I turn to look at him, a grin tipping my lips. A chorus of "You were beat by a chick," "Way to go, Stacy," "Dude," and something about being whipped are all thrown out at once.

"She's good. Didn't even lift in the corners."

"Damn, girl!" Tristan stands, heads toward me, and Cole throws his arm over my shoulders. For some reason, this causes Tristan to grin like a fool.

"She's a tiny thing," he says softly, his eyes holding mine.

"Riiight," Gavin says, standing. "Let's go before I die of starvation."

With a quick wave, they're out the door and it's just the two of us yet again.

CHAPTER 27

"WATCH A MOVIE WITH ME?" I ask as soon as the door closes, not ready for my time with her to end. I've loved every fucking minute of today.

"You can watch whatever," she says, placing her hand over her mouth to hide her yawn. "I'll probably just fall asleep, but I'll sit with you for a while."

Victory! I kick off my shoes and stretch out on the couch. The way I see it, we have at least a couple hours before everyone gets back, so I'll lie with her until she falls asleep. I'm not even going to try to seduce her; we've had a long day, not to mention holding her sounds really fucking good right now.

I pat the couch in front of me; she hesitates for a few seconds before kicking off her own shoes and lying down. I pull the throw blanket off the back, something that was never on a bus of ours in the past. Not until the girls came along. In the past, our assistants traveled with the crew. Not this time.

I pull the blanket over us and reach for the remote. I turn on some movie, no idea what it is. It doesn't matter, though, because neither one of us are going to be watching it. She won't last ten minutes, and I'd rather watch her. Shocking, but true.

I set the remote on the floor and wrap my arm around her. She's using the other as a pillow.

"I had fun today," she says sleepily.

"Me too," I reply, keeping my voice soft and low.

"Did you let me win?"

I chuckle. "No, sweets. I didn't let you win. You're kind of badass."

"Hmmm."

My hand caresses the small of her back. I slip my fingers underneath her shirt, needing to feel her skin. It's a need I can't explain.

"I like this."

"What?" Her voice is getting softer.

"You, in my arms." I liked every fucking second of our time together today, and every day before that.

"Me too. This is my favorite." She's completely relaxed, lying in my arms.

"You're my favorite." It's the same thought that has been running through my mind lately. She's different. She's a blast to be around, beautiful, sexy, smart—she's the entire fucking package. She's a damn unicorn and she's in my arms right now.

"Hmmm."

That's her reply. I kiss the top of her head and relax into the couch, which is surprisingly comfortable considering. It has to be her. It's all her. Every day I wake up, it's her; before I fall asleep, it's her. On stage, events, hanging with the guys . . . it's all her.

I tighten my hold on her as realization kicks in. I want to try with her. I want to try to be her more. It's something I've never wanted, never imagined I would ever want. Now that it's here in my arms, it's easy to see.

She's everything.

My mind races with the possibilities. I remember the pang of envy I felt at Kacen and Logan's wedding. She could be my someone. I want her to be. There's something about the tightening in my chest at just the thought of her that tells me this is right. Now I just have to convince her that it's more.

My past follows me, but even she admitted that this tour is not what she expected. And it hasn't been the usual, that's for sure. I know my reasoning, not sure about Gavin and Tristan. I know I'm a man consumed.

She's all I see.

Now, I just have to figure out how to prove to her that she's not like the rest.

"Shh, leave them be," I hear Logan scolding my bandmates.

We fell asleep again and once again are busted. I slow smile pulls at my lips.

"That fucker's awake," Tristan whines.

I open my eyes to find the four of them standing over us. Bringing my index finger to my lips, I reiterate what Logan was saying, telling them to be quiet. Kacen is grinning like a fool, Tristan looks confused, and Gavin's phone has his attention.

"You got her?" Kacen asks.

I wrap my arm back around her and meet his stare. No words are exchanged, but he knows. He's been there—hell, he *is* there. I know he can see it. I'm not leaving this fucking couch as long as she's in my arms.

He nods, and then, reaching over, he turns the light over the table off and heads back toward the bedroom. Tristan and Gavin follow blindly, like they don't understand what's happening.

They've never seen me like this, but they're smart guys. They have to know what this means.

Closing my eyes, I listen as they all get settled in for the night. After a few minutes of silence, I shift so Stacy is lying on top of me. My arm is asleep.

She moves to find a comfortable position, her eyes never opening. I hold her close and allow my own eyes to close.

It takes hours for sleep to claim me again; I don't want to miss a minute of this. I want this girl like nothing ever before, and I don't know that I can convince her of that. I will put everything I am into showing her she's more.

Until then, while she's sleeping, I'll bask in the fact that she's where she is. Next to me, her head resting on my heart. My arms holding her close.

It feels like a dream, having her with me like this. It's new, and already I'm addicted. She's my drug of choice.

CHAPTER 28

Stacy

"SPILL." MY BEST FRIEND IS standing in front of the small table on the bus, hands on her hips, small baby bump front and center, giving me the look. You know, the one that says, "Do not deny your pregnant hormonal best friend or there will be hell to pay."

It's been two weeks since I woke up wrapped around Cole on the couch here on the bus. Two weeks of non-stop running and organizing for the tour. That stretch of fourteen days, they played seven of them. It was constant, exhausting and life-saving all at once, since I was able to avoid Logan and her questioning. Any time she would start to ask, one of the guys would interrupt us, one of our phones would ring, or we were backstage.

Until now.

Finally, we get a break that is more than one day off in a stretch. We get four. Four entire days to do with as we wish. Sure, Logan and I will have a few things to take care of here and there—confirming security, location clearance, things like that. But between the two of us, we can knock that out in no time.

"There's not really anything to spill," I tell her honestly. I'm just as confused as she is.

"I call bullshit. He's always touching you, and you two spend all your spare time together. What gives?" She slides into the table across from me.

"Honestly, I don't know what's going on. For months he pursued me, told me how great we would be together. The last few weeks, he's been different. I barely get a sexual innuendo from him, and if I do, it's backed up with something that only sweet Cole would say and I'm all mushy inside. Too mushy to care that he propositioned me for sex."

"Sweet Cole?" She grins.

"Yes! The man, I swear, it's like he has a microphone that goes straight to my heart. Some of the things he says. . . ."

"Like?" she prompts.

I don't want to reveal too much—not because I don't trust her, but I don't know what it all means. Hell, it could all be in my head. She knows him pretty well, though, so it could be nice to get her opinion. Decision made, I give her an example. "Okay, that night we fell asleep." I point over my shoulder to the couch, and she nods. "He said that lying like that was nice. Then he told me I was his favorite." It was more than that, the way he said it. I might have been half asleep, but it didn't make the effect on me any less profound.

"I literally melted into him," I confess.

"He's into you."

That's it? He's into me? "I kinda already know that, but what does the rest of it mean?"

"He's never been in a relationship."

"I know that too."

This information causes a surprised look to cross her face. "Sounds like it's more serious than I thought."

"Logan!"

She laughs. Fucking *laughs*.

"Look, Cole is a great guy. He's an open book, and he will never lie to you, but he doesn't easily open up in regards to personal stuff. Not unless he trusts you."

"Will you just spit it out already?" I ask, exasperated.

"Kace says you're his Logan."

Holy shit!

"He's. . . . That's not. . . . He doesn't do that." I struggle to find the words.

"He didn't used to. Not because he's damaged or been burned. It was just never something he thought he wanted. My guess is that he found something . . . some*one* who made him change his mind."

Just as I'm about to debate, the door to the bus opens and in rolls Soul Serenade. Cole heads straight to me, sliding in beside me in the booth. His arm goes on the back of the seat before he leans down and kisses my shoulder.

"Hey." He winks.

"You all are back early," Logan comments.

"These two"—Gavin points to Cole and Kacen—"couldn't be away from their women any longer. We decided to put them out of their misery and stop here to get a bite to eat before heading into the stadium."

His comment doesn't seem to faze either one of them.

"How was your day?" Cole's lips are next to my ear.

Kacen and Logan are already in their own conversation, while Gavin and Tristan are digging in the cabinets.

"Good, it was nice to just hang out. So, what's left to do for the day?"

"Just need to clean out our stuff from the room from the show last night. We did two radio spots this morning. After that, we're done for four long days. I've missed hanging out with you." He nudges my knee with his.

"Hey," Logan says, getting our attention. "We've been talking." She motions between her and Kacen. "What do you all think about finding a hotel and crashing for a few nights? Sleep in a full-size bed for a change."

I watch as Kacen whispers something in her ear that causes her to blush.

A resounding yes comes from all of us.

"Stacy, do you mind calling to book the rooms?" Kacen asks.

"Sure. Any specifics?"

"Nope, just make sure they understand the privacy."

"Got it, I'll use my first name and just pick one of your last names for the reservation."

"Mine," Cole says beside me.

"You mind if I use your room to make the reservation? I don't want to sound like I'm with a bunch of rock stars."

Cole rises, allowing me to stand up. He starts to follow me, but I stop him. "I got this. Eat something."

"You want anything?"

"No, thank you, though." With that, I close the bedroom door. Well, it's more of a really small closet with a bed that takes up the entire floor space. A hotel room sounds like pure Heaven right now.

I pull up the spreadsheet Cassidy created with hotels in every city. They're all prepared to go to great lengths to have our identity remain secret just to announce that we stayed there after we've already gone.

Picking one, I dial the number. "Hi, I would like to make a reservation." It only takes a few minutes once I announce who I am, and I reserve everything under Stacy Hampton.

Cole will love that.

"All set," I state, joining them in the kitchen.

"Great, pack what you need, ladies," Tristan says.

"Yeah, get what you need, babe. You guys can go with us to the stadium."

"Don't you have people for that?" I ask.

This causes all of them to break out in a fit of laughter.

"We do, but we like to do it. We like to make sure nothing is left behind."

"I'm getting cheated," I mumble.

"What's that, sweets?" Cole asks.

Of course he would hear me. "Nothing,"

"How are you getting cheated?" Gavin questions.

I can feel my face heat with embarrassment. "You all are not rock stars."

"We're not?" Tristan asks.

"No! Where are the parties and the groupies and the people waiting on you hand and foot?" I'm genuinely asking. This is not what the media portrays them to be, or all of the others for that matter.

"Sorry to disappoint," Kacen says, laughing.

"No, it's not necessarily that I'm disappointed, just confused. The media acts like you all are man-whores and divas all rolled into one."

"Well, we *are* man-whores. Don't let the last month fool you. The three of us have had our fair share," Gavin explains. "This one"—he points to Cole—"is stuck on you." Again, I feel the blush. "I can't speak for Tristan, but I've been busy with the label and learning what I can. I'm excited on where the future might lead us." That's what he says, but I can tell he's leaving something out. Something important.

"I'm just not into it." Tristan shrugs. "I guess we all grow up eventually."

I want to call bullshit, but instead, let it drop. Besides, my face already looks like a damn tomato.

"Get packed. You can go with us and we'll head straight to the hotel."

I don't argue; instead, I pack a bag, throwing in toiletries and clothes for a couple of days.

"Don't worry about forgetting anything. We're going to get the crew rooms too. The bus will be close by."

"Do you want me to call and arrange it?" I ask.

"No, Kacen is having Cassidy take care of it. The label will cover it."

I throw a few more things in my bag and zip it up.

"You forgot something, babe," he says with a smile.

"What's that?"

Leaning down, he reaches into my cubby and pulls out my Kindle charger. "Thought you might want to take this too."

Really? As if he doesn't make my heart race on a normal day, sweet Cole has to go and remember my Kindle charger. Most men would bitch about their girl "reading all the damn time."

"Thank you."

He nods, and I stand and wait for him while he throws a few things into a bag. Once he's finished, he reaches out and takes mine from me. "I'll have the crew load this up."

So I guess I'm getting to see a little of the "spoiled rock star," but this is still not at all what I expected.

CHAPTER 29

I MANAGED TO FOLD MY six-foot-four self into the back of our Suburban. Gavin likes to drive, Tristan called shotgun, and Kacen, of course, wanted to sit with his wife. Not that I'm complaining; I'm not going to make the pregnant girl climb into the back, of course. So here I sit, with Stacy squished beside me. I couldn't have planned it better if I'd tried. The radio is up, so each of us are having our own conversations.

"You're all scrunched." She giggles

I rub my thumb across her knuckles; I can't be this close to her and not be touching her. She never resists anymore.

"I'm not complaining. I'm scrunched with you."

"I guess you think that's a good thing?"

"I do. So tell me, what do you want to do the next couple of days?"

"Cole, it's your time off. You've been working nonstop. Go out, have some fun."

Here we go. Not exactly how I wanted to have this conversation, but it needs to finally happen. I slouch in the seat and pull her close to me. She's facing away from me, but my arms are wrapped around her. My lips next to her ear, I start to talk.

"Stacy, I want to be your more. I want to try this with you. I haven't touched—hell, *looked* at another woman in months. You consume me. I want you to be my girl. I want to give this a go, see if we can make this work." I kiss the top of her head.

She doesn't respond for a long time. Finally, she looks up at me, those green eyes putting me under her spell. "This is real to me, Cole."

Fuck! This is not where or how I wanted to do this. I move to sit up and she does the same; her back against the seat, I lean over and block us from the view of our friends. I gently cup her face, feeling her soft skin. "Baby, I've never been more real about anything in my life. I want this. I want you. I don't know what the hell I'm doing, but whatever it is, being in a relationship, all of that, I want it with you."

She bites down on her lip and her eyes fill with tears. I'm just about to take it all back, to tell her we can do what we've been doing, anything to stop her tears. Until she nods.

"Baby?"

"Okay," she whispers, as if she's still uncertain. "Don't break my heart, Cole."

Never.

Leaning in, I kiss her, just a soft touch of my lips to hers. I feel tears on my lips.

"Don't cry, sweets. We're going to rock this. You and me, okay?"

"Okay," she says again.

Fuck, I sound like I'm giving her a fucking pep talk before a damn basketball game. She's going to dump my dumb ass before we get started.

"We'll take it as fast or as slow as you want, but I want you to be mine. Above all else, I need to know that you're mine." I know with all that I am that we will make this work. Failing her, these feelings I have for her, is not an option.

"Okay," she repeats. This time, a slow smile graces her lips.

She's mine. That was easier than I thought, but then again, I've been showing her every fucking day that she's all I see.

We pull into the hotel and the paparazzi are ready and waiting. Someone tipped them off, and I'm sure it was Brian fucking Wilson, none other than the CEO of Stone Records.

"Fucking Brian," Kacen seethes. He's pissed too.

We want a few nights to just be us. Most of the time, people will leave us alone if we don't roll in a huge entourage. Unless someone tips them off. We've had a feeling it's been Brian for a while now. It all traces back to him. Jones wouldn't do that; he's one of the good guys.

"Stacy, I need you to stay close to me. The valet will take care of the car and our bags, so just grab your purse and stay close."

She nods. I climb over her and get out first, wanting to shield her from them as much as possible. Not because I want to hide her, but because I just got her to agree to try this with me. I don't need them digging into her life and scaring her away before I have a chance to convince her that we're good together.

Once I'm out, I reach in for her hand. The others are already inside. When she steps out, I wrap my arms around her and she buries her head in my chest.

"Cole, over here."

"Who's the girl?"

"Is she your girlfriend?"

"Cole, can we get a picture."

I ignore every single one of them. All I want to do is get Stacy inside. Everyone else is waiting for us just inside the door. Security is keeping the paparazzi out.

"You all right, sweets?" I kiss her temple.

"Yeah." She smiles up at me.

"What did we miss?" Logan asks.

I look down at the stunning woman in my arms and smirk. She gives a small nod; she knows what I'm asking.

I kiss her temple one more time before facing our friends, my family. These three guys and Logan are my extended family, and I'm bursting with both anxiety and excitement to tell them.

"I convinced this one"—I pull her to my chest—"to be my girl."

I expect a chorus of "No shit." Or "What are you thinking?" for Stacy. Instead, we're met with knowing smiles.

"Finally, you both realize it. I thought we were going to have to dumb it down for the two of you." Gavin says.

"What?" Stacy asks.

"Stacy, we all could see it. You two don't take your eyes off each other. We were just letting you come to the conclusion on your own. Although, Gavin's right. We thought we were going to have to point it out," Logan tells us.

Stacy giggles beside me and I want to bottle the sound.

A hotel attendant approaches us. "Mrs. Hampton?" He looks at Stacy, because well, everyone knows Kace and Logan are married.

She used my name. I want to beat on my chest like a fucking caveman. It sounds pretty fucking fantastic too.

Stacy Hampton.

Mrs. Cole Hampton

I like it.

"You used my name," I say next to her ear.

Looking over her shoulder at me, she smiles. "You told me to."

"Here are your keys, ma'am. As we discussed on the phone, I already checked you in. The valet will handle your car and deliver your bags . . . Uh, we might not know whose go where." The girl looks scared that we're going to rip her head off.

"No problem. Just drop them off in any of the rooms and we can sort it out from there," Stacy tells her.

"Yes, ma'am. Take the elevator to the top floor. All the suites on that floor are yours." She hands her room cards.

In the elevator, Stacy hands everyone a key but me, and I don't question her. I assume she wants to talk about this revelation in the car before we go our separate ways. If I had my way, I would never leave her side. My room can set empty for all I care.

That's a first for me.

The elevator ride is quiet. I think everyone is just excited for a full-sized bed and a good night's sleep that doesn't have anything to do with a noisy, bumpy interstate.

We reach the top floor and scatter our separate ways. I follow Stacy to what I assume is her room. She inserts the card and I follow her inside.

Once the door closes, she turns to face me. She's biting her lip and looks worried about something. My heart drops instantly—she's changed her mind. I knew I wanted this, being more with her. It's not until this moment that I realize that *I* want it—not just to give her what she wants, but for me too.

I want her.

I step forward and wrap my arms around her. "What's wrong?"

"I didn't get you a room," she says. She sounds worried.

"No problem, I can call down and get it fixed or room with one of the guys." I would offer to stay with her, because that's where I want to be, but she looks too worried for that. I don't want to push her for fear of her telling me to hit the road. I'll try to rationalize my need to be next to her another time.

"No, I did it on purpose. I thought you could stay with me."

Hell fucking yes! I pick her up and swing her around. "Good choice, beautiful," I say as my lips cover hers.

All too soon, she's breaking the kiss. "Cole, put me down." She laughs.

"Wrap your legs around me," I tell her before kissing her again.

For weeks, I've been this softer version of myself. I knew then, even though I wouldn't have admitted it, that this is how I wanted to end up. Her in my arms. I've enjoyed actually taking the time to get to know her, but she agreed to be mine. It's now my mission to prove to her that taking a chance on me—on *us*—was the right decision.

"Cole," she breathes as I trail kisses down her neck.

"You want this," I rasp.

"Yes."

It's great that she isn't fighting me on it, but it wasn't a question. I can feel her heat. I know she wants this, wants me. And I plan to deliver.

When I grip her ass, she breaks the kiss and buries her head in my neck. In two strides, I have her pressed against the wall, my body molded against hers.

"I need those lips, sweets," I rasp in her ear.

Without hesitation, her lips cover mine as she works her hands up to my hair and removes the tie. She immediately grabs on as she deepens the kiss. She's sweet, like honey.

Hands still on her ass, I pull her against me. She gasps when she feels my hard cock against her heat. I lean in to kiss her again, but stop when she rotates her hips against mine.

Fuck me.

"Stacy." Her name is the only word I can get past my lips as she rolls her hips again.

"More," she pants.

More.

I quickly walk us to the bed, setting her on the edge. She keeps her legs wrapped around my waist and I lean over her, my arms resting on either side of her head. When she lifts her hips, I fight against the moan sitting in the back of my throat.

Placing all my weight on one hand, careful not to crush her, the other gently grips her chin, making her look at me. "I need to hear you say it."

She smirks. "It."

"Smartass." I grin as I lean down and kiss the corner of her mouth.

"What do you want to hear Cole? That I've fought my attraction to you for months? That I'm willing to throw away my idea of dating and future for a chance to be with you? Do you want me to tell you that the reward of feeling you inside me is worth the risk of a broken heart?" She cups my face. "Or maybe you want me to tell you that I'm wet for you? That you're driving me crazy and I want you inside me? Is that what you want to hear?" Her voice is softer now.

"All of the above," I say against her lips.

"Cole." My name is a whisper from her lips. Pulling back, my eyes meet hers. "Don't break me."

My heart is pounding against my chest. Break her? I want to fucking cherish her. But Kace is the one with the words, not me. How do I make her understand?

"You're beautiful," I tell her. Her emerald eyes are shining bright.

I watch as her face turns a light shade of pink. "It," she says with a soft smile.

I nod once. I know what she wants. Standing to my full height, I pull my shirt over my head and toss it across the room. Stacy sits up and does the same. I want to be the one stripping her, but I'm man enough to admit that if I do, this is going to be over before it starts.

I don't take my eyes off her as she reaches behind her back and removes her bra. Sliding one strap off then the other, she slowly lets it fall before tossing it behind her. Lying back against the bed, she unbuttons her jeans, lifts her hips, and shimmies them down her thighs, along with her thong. I take over from there, pulling them down her legs and tossing them to the side.

"Your turn."

Sitting up, her hands immediately begin to unbutton my jeans. Slowly, she lowers the zipper, and then I step away from her and kick them off. I went commando today, so my cock stands proud . . . for her.

My eyes find hers and she's licking her lips. I send up a silent prayer that I won't embarrass myself.

Without a word, she turns and climbs up on the bed. She settles on her back, right in the middle. Stepping forward, I take her in. Her long locks are spread out on the pillow, emerald eyes filled with heat, pink pouty lips, and a body any man would die to be able to worship.

"I've waited so long for this," I say. My voice is husky against the desire that's coursing through me.

I need to be inside her.

As I start to climb on the bed, I remember—protection.

I stalk away to find my jeans.

"Cole?"

I dig around until I find my wallet and pull out the condom. I raise it in the air and show her what I'm doing; she relaxes back into the soft mattress. At least it looks soft, but then again, maybe it's just her. Stacy makes anything look soft. Just look at what she's done to me.

In two long strides, I'm back at the bed. I crawl on from the bottom, taking in the beauty before me, pause only long enough to rip open the condom and quickly roll it on. I continue on until I'm nestled between her thighs.

"Why did you stop?" she asks breathlessly.

I haven't even touched her yet. "I need to make sure you're ready for me."

"I'm good," she assures me.

"You sure?" I quirk a brow.

Her answer is to raise her hips and search for me, and I have to fight like hell not to slide inside her. I pull my hips back and rest my weight on one arm; the other's searching out the answer. Sure enough, I find her soaked.

"Told you." She smirks.

I don't even try to hold in the laugh that escapes my lips. "That you did," I say, placing my weight on both elbows on either side of her head. Reaching up, I smooth the hair away from her face. "You good?" I ask as I rub my cock against her center.

"Not yet," she pants. "But I will be." She runs her fingers through my hair and pulls me closer, pressing her lips against mine.

I get lost in the kiss, in the duel of my tongue with hers. I drink in the taste of her. I want to kiss every inch of her ivory skin.

Next time.

There will most certainly be a next time, and that's when I will devour every fucking inch of her. Right now, I need to be inside her.

Again, she raises her hips, and that's when it happens. I slide home.

Home.

I freeze.

She feels like heaven. She feels like home. It hits me like a lightning bolt—this is more for me because I'm falling in love with her.

Hell, I think I might already love her.

CHAPTER 30

A MOAN THAT WOULD PUT a porn star to shame falls from my lips the minute he pushes inside me.

Then he stops.

I watch as he stares down at me, a look I can't quite describe on his face.

"Cole," I say hesitantly.

"I won't ever," he replies reverently.

I run my fingers through his hair. "You've lost me," I tell him.

He lowers himself so there is not one part of him that's not touching me. "I won't break you."

He's responding to what I said earlier.

Don't break me.

His voice doesn't waver, his statement bold and confident.

Assured.

It's obvious that this is a declaration on his part. A promise not to break my heart. I'm at a loss for words. What do I say to that? Okay? I'm going to hold you to it? I can't seem to find my voice as the sentiment of his words sink in. Instead, I smile softly and pull him closer for a kiss, slowly moving my lips with his, enjoying the feel of his weight against me.

When I do find my voice, the only word that comes to mind is "It."

Cole chuckles as he slowly rocks his hips against mine.

"I'm going to have to apologize now."

"What are you talking about?" I laugh. I've never been with a guy where you can be funny and serious in such an intimate situation.

"I'm not going to last, babe." He rocks his hips again. I watch as he clenches his eyes closed.

"You can make it up to me next time." I lean up and kiss his shoulder. He starts a steady rhythm, and I meet him stroke for stroke. "It's . . . not going to take long," I pant as he does this . . . swirling, thrusting thing with his hips that hits all the right spots.

"Never fucking felt like this," he vows. He stops moving as his lips capture mine. I immediately open for him. I get lost in the kiss as his tongue stokes mine. He's all consuming.

Breaking away from this kiss, his lips trail down my neck nipping and sucking along the way. When his warm mouth captures a nipple, I arch my back off the bed.

"More," I plead. My hands grip his ass as I try to pull him into me. He releases my nipple with a pop and moves right over to the other, giving it equal amounts of his attention, ignoring my plea. I'm on fire. I can feel every stroke of his tongue, the touch of his fingers as they dig into my hips, his weight against me. He's turning my body into liquid fire, lava.

"Cole," I whimper.

He pulls back and stares down at me. His eyes, dark brown pools of desire lock on mine. "So fucking sweet," he whispers as his lips once again descend on mine.

My heart literally skips a beat. I'm overwhelmed with emotions—fear, elation, passion and desire. All of them because of the man above me.

"Are you with me, sweets?"

"Yes," I say, gripping his back. Holding on for the ride. One I know I'll want to experience over and over again.

Cole locks his fingers at the top of my head, his weight resting on his elbows as enters me slowly. Each thrust of his hips is calculated and sure. His eyes never leave mine as he gives me exactly what I've been begging for, more of this, more of him.

Closing my eyes, I try to hide from the intensity of his stare.

"Open your eyes, Stacy. I want to watch you. I want you to watch me. I want you to remember this moment, remember who's inside of you."

I should have known that I couldn't hide from him. Cole doesn't hide he's a "what you see is what you get" kind of guy.

"There you are," he murmurs. Leaning down his lips softly caress mine.

"Cole." His name is but a whisper on my lips.

"I can feel it," he rocks his hips. "You're close," he sways his hips in a move that causes my entire body to tremble.

"Close," I pant.

Cole doesn't say anything. His eyes remain locked on mine. Resting all of his weight on one elbow the other hand cups my cheek. His eyes darken as I bite my lip; his hips jolt forward, his thrust growing faster, a constant steady rhythm that is pushing me toward the edge.

Just as my eyes are about to roll back in my head, he thrust deep and slams his lips over mine. He swallows my cries as we both fall into the abyss of pleasure that we have created.

He kisses me, his lips fused with mine until the last tremor has left our bodies, slowly he pulls his lips from mine. His eyes watch me searching my expression, looking for I don't know what.

"Regrets?" he asks softly.

"No," I murmur. "You?"

Leaning down, he kisses my forehead. "Could never regret you, baby."

Five words. Those five words have a direct line to my heart. The one this man kicks into overdrive whenever he's near. The one that just melted into a puddle of goo at five little words. Those five words mean more to me than any declaration of love or feelings. Cole is a man who doesn't hold back; he's always blunt and honest to a fault. He knows I want more than just a fling, knows how I feel about it. He also knows I was willing to set that aside to be with him. Those five words tell me that this really does mean more to him.

We're in this together.

That both excites me and scares the hell out of me. This isn't his thing, being attached to someone. Although, I've yet to see his attention anywhere but on me. I agreed to try, and that's what I'm going to do.

"Where did you go?" he asks, smoothing hair out of my eyes.

"Just taking it all in." I smile.

"Don't move."

He climbs off the bed and I instantly miss him, the warmth of him pressed against me. I close my eyes, running it all through my mind on repeat. We've been dancing around this for months, and I've imagined it more times than I care to admit, but I never, not once, thought it would be like this. With Cole saying he wants there to be an us.

My eyes pop open when I feel a warm cloth between my legs.

"Sorry, sweets. Didn't mean to startle you," he says, tossing the towel back toward the bathroom. He stretches out beside me on the bed, pulling me against his chest. Reaching down, he grabs the covers and tugs them over us.

My head resting on his chest, I can feel the thunderous beat of his heart. Neither one of us says a word as our breathing syncs and we both relax.

Cole has one arm holding me tight against him, and with the other he runs his fingers through my hair. "I've never done this before," he admits.

"Changing your mind?" I ask hesitantly.

"Never." He tightens both arms around me and holds me tight. He gives me a gentle squeeze. "I've never . . . cuddled after sex."

Noted. I try to pull away, but his hold is like a vise.

"Stop."

I do what he says.

"I didn't say I didn't want to do it, Stacy. I said I'd never. I've never wanted to. I've never had the desire to stick around, to bask in the feel of a naked body against mine. I've never cared enough to make sure she's comfortable."

It's a bit awkward hearing about his time with other women, but that's Cole. He doesn't hold any punches, and I know his history.

"Fuck, sweets, I never want to let you go. This feeling—your skin against mine, your head on my chest. It's one I never want to let go of."

Me either. I want to tell him that I'm onboard, that my thoughts are in line with his, but I hold back. This is still so new, and I admit that I'm still scared as hell. If I let sweet Cole in, will he break me?

"This is more, Stacy," he states firmly, as if he can read my mind.

"Not just sex," I say, snuggling closer. I'm going to soak up as much of him as I can. I'm going to take my clues from him and let the chips fall where they may. I want to believe he's changed, that he changed for me, but my heart is hesitant. It's his simple "this is more" that has me going all in I'm not going to let my fear of a broken heart keep me from enjoying every second that he claims to be mine.

"No, not just sex. Look at me," he commands.

Taking a deep breath, I lift my head from what I like to think of as my spot on his chest and look at him.

His face is serious, more serious than I've ever seen. Those chocolate eyes bore into mine. "We made love, Stacy. I could never just fuck the woman who owns me. We'll fuck, that's a given, but there will always be emotion involved—there's no other way with you. However, what we just shared, that was more than sex."

Love. That one word among the many that fell from his lips is the one I'm stuck on. I bite my tongue, not wanting to blurt it out that it was more than making love—it was falling in love as well. That my heart is invested. Sweet Cole has cast a spell on me, and my heart was all too eager to succumb to his advances.

"Stacy."

I pull myself together and focus on him.

"Tell me you get that?" His voice is pleading.

"I do," I murmur. "We made love," I rasp out.

He nods and I lay my head back on his chest, breaking the intensity of his stare.

"I want to wake up like this," he says on a yawn.

This man. No one would believe me. If I told them about sweet Cole and the things he says to me, the way he holds me firm yet gentle. No one would believe that rocker Cole Hampton, lead guitarist for Soul

Serenade, is the man holding me tight, vowing to do so all night long.

I like that.

I like the idea that I get the real Cole. A side of him the groupies and the fans don't get to see. I get all of him—the cocky rocker, the loveable uncle, and the man who goes out of his way to make sure I know he just made love to me. Something we both know is another first for him.

I get my Cole.

"Morning, beautiful," Cole's sleepy voice rasps in my ear.

I slowly open my eyes and search for his. As promised, I'm still in his arms. "Morning," I say, placing my hand over my mouth. I don't want to knock him out with morning breath.

"Where are you going?" He holds tight when I try to get up.

I can't help but laugh at his expression. He looks worried. "I have to pee and brush my teeth."

"I need a kiss," he begs. Yes, *begs*. It's cute as hell, and no one would ever believe me.

"After I brush my teeth."

"Now."

He reaches for me, but I quickly roll away from him and climb out of bed. "Trust me on this one. This is new to you. Morning-breath kisses are not something you want to experience."

"It is if it's with you," he pouts.

I just shake my head at his antics and rush to the bathroom before I lose control of my bladder. Just as I finish washing my hands, Cole barges into the room. He relieves himself as if I'm not even there.

I leave the bathroom to find my suitcase, but the luggage isn't there.

Shit.

I stalk back to the bathroom. I'll just have to use my finger with the sample that the hotel gives you. I find Cole at the sink, doing that very thing. He flashes me a grin.

"I wonder what the hotel did with our luggage," I say, picking up the toothpaste.

"I'd say the others have it."

"Why didn't they call or bring it to us?"

He winks at me. "They know we're together. They saw you hand everyone a key but me."

I was so wrapped up in Cole that I didn't even think about the others and what they might be noticing.

"It's no big deal. We're solid." He slaps me on the ass as he leaves the room.

I finish brushing my teeth as best I can before joining him. He stalks toward me and, before I have time to resist, his lips are on mine. Gentle yet firm, he kisses me until there is a knock at the door.

"The newlyweds have our luggage," he says against my lips. He pulls away and tosses his phone on the bed. "Sweets, you need to either hide in the bathroom or throw on a robe or clothes or something." He runs his fingers through his hair, gathering it together and pulling it into a knot at the back of his head.

The knock sounds again. "Cole, you said you were awake," Kace calls through the door.

"Hold your damn horses," Cole yells back. He turns to me, "Stacy, you need to get moving." He smirks.

He knows I was checking him out. Nothing but his jeans on, and unbuttoned at that. His ripped chest on display.

"I'm just going to get in the shower."

"Don't come out until you know they're gone."

"It's not like. . . ."

"Not with you. No one gets to see you but me." He kisses me hard one last time and smacks my ass for the second time this morning. I yelp in surprise and scurry off to the bathroom.

CHAPTER 31

COLE

IT'S HARD TO BELIEVE THAT there are only four weeks of the tour left. I spent the first four chasing my girl and the last four enjoying every minute of her being mine. This week, we have a show in Cincinnati. Luckily, we have three days off after, so we're going to spend some time at Logan and Kacen's house here before hitting the road again. Logan is beaming that she gets to see her family. I guess Jase, her younger brother, is coming home from college for a few days. Apparently, he explained to all his professors that his sister, who is married to a rock star, is coming into town. Not that they would give him shit anyway; he's the big man on campus, football star and all. We need to make it to a game sometime. I need to mention that to Kace; I'm sure Logan would be thrilled. Of course, with the baby due in just two months, not sure if it will be this season.

Lots of changes going on, for sure.

I know my relationship with Stacy is one of them. Kacen has finally accepted it. After that first night I spent with her, he asked me if I was sure about what I was doing—always the sensible one. Once I told him that Stacy was my Logan, he hasn't said another word.

I check the time on my cell phone. The girls were supposed to be here fifteen minutes ago, and those two are the most punctual women I've ever met.

"I just talked to Logan," Kacen tells me. "Apparently, she's 'dragging ass' and they're on their way." He smiles.

"She doing okay?"

"Yeah, as she gets further along, she gets tired easily."

"How about you, man?"

"Never fucking better." He grins.

"Excited about meeting the little guy?" Gavin asks.

"You know he's going to play the drums, right?" Tristan asks.

Kacen and Logan found out they're having a boy the day after I spent my first night with Stacy. To say that Kacen is ecstatic is an understatement.

"Hell yes, I am. I can't wait to meet him. And he can play whatever the hell he wants," he adds. "Besides, you play more than one instrument."

Tristan is like a fucking musical genius. He plays piano, drums, guitar, and can rock a harmonica like nobody's business.

"True story." Tristan laughs.

The sound of the chaos outside our dressing room filters in. Turning toward the door, I see two bodyguards escorting the girls safely into our room.

Conversation lost, Kacen and I seek them out. I wrap my arms around Stacy and she relaxes into me. Her hold is weak. "What's wrong?"

"Just not feeling well."

I pull back and place my hand on her forehead, like I know what I'm doing. I have no fucking clue, but it's what my mom used to do when Chloe and I were kids. I've seen Chloe and Kyle do the same with Mia. She feels warm, but does she have a fever? Fuck if I know.

"Can I get you anything?"

"Just you," she says, resting her head back against my chest.

Undone. Never thought I would want to be spouting words of love and shit, but this girl . . . She changes everything.

"That I can do," I affirm. Resting my chin on her head, I hold her close.

A roadie raps on the door. "Showtime."

"You okay to watch the show?" I ask, my lips next to her ear.

"Of course. I wouldn't miss it."

I motion for the guard who stays with her to lead us backstage. There are people everywhere, including the paparazzi. Now that it's out that she's taken me off the market, they're like vultures trying to get pictures of us.

We make it backstage and there are two stools waiting where they always are. Far enough back that the crowd can't see them, but close enough that we can.

I lean in to kiss her and she turns her head. "I don't know if I'm coming down with something. I don't want to get you sick."

I don't like it, but I get it. I settle for a kiss to her temple before taking my place onstage.

The crowd is full of energy. They go wild when Kacen tells them the love of his life is a Buckeye.

Every time I look over at Stacy, she's just sitting, tapping her foot to the beat. Logan isn't her usual peppy self either. I'm glad we have a few days off so the girls can get some rest. I watch as Kacen keeps checking on them as well.

How things have changed.

As soon as the lights go down after our second encore, I'm handing off my guitar and heading toward her. She stands when she sees me, a soft smile on her face.

I wrap my arm around her shoulders. "Let's get you out of here."

"I got it, man," Gavin says. He looks from me to Stacy.

I nod my thanks, happy I don't have to worry about making sure my stuff is packed up. It doesn't matter anyway—I already have what's most important with me.

I don't go back to the room; instead, accompanied by the bodyguard, I take my girl back to the bus. We're taking it to Kacen's. We set the crew up in a hotel for the next few days, and the driver will take a cab back to the hotel as well.

The driver is waiting for us once we reach the bus, and he unlocks the door then holds it open for us. Just as he's about to shut it, I hear,

"Wait up." Turning, I see that Kacen and Logan had the same idea.

I lead Stacy to the couch and she sits, resting her head against the wall. "What do you need, sweets?" I kneel in front of her and gently rub her thighs.

"Some Advil, maybe?" Logan says from behind me.

Stacy nods.

I jump into action, rummaging through the cabinet in the bathroom until I find a bottle and let three pills fall into my palm. I grab a cold bottle of water from the fridge and kneel before her once again.

"Take these." I hand her the pills and open the bottle of water, passing it to her as well.

"Thank you," she croaks out.

This is the first thing she's said since the show ended, and she sounds terrible.

I look over at the table where Kacen and Logan are sitting. "What can I do?"

"Sore throat?" Logan asks, and Stacy nods. "Headache?" Another nod. "Body aches?" another nod. "She probably has strep throat. She gets it every year, and it usually starts like this."

"We need to take her to the emergency room." I stand, ready to carry her there if I have to.

"No, we don't. An urgent care or one of those pharmacy clinics is fine. She does need to see a doctor to get some antibiotics, though." Logan starts typing on her phone. "Okay, so the urgent care on the way back to the house is open until eleven."

"What time is it now?" It has to be getting close to that. We didn't go on until eight, and our set it two hours long.

"It's ten thirty."

"How far is it from here?"

"There's one around the corner," Kacen chimes in, showing us his phone screen. "They close at eleven as well."

I'm just about to call a cab when Gavin and Tristan climb on board, carrying all of our stuff. "Clyde," I address the driver. Kacen rattles off the address as Clyde takes his place behind the wheel.

Kace was right; the urgent care is literally right around the corner from the venue. Stacy stands, and I bend down and pick her up in my arms.

"I can walk," she squeaks out.

"Shh, I know you can, but you don't have to. I got you." I carry her from the bus with Gavin hot on my heels. He gets the door for me. I set Stacy in a chair, and Gavin takes the seat beside her. The receptionist at the window immediately recognizes me.

"OH, MY GOD!" she screams, and I cringe. "I can't believe it's you. I wanted to go to your show but I couldn't get off work. This is so much better. EEEK! Gavin too!"

I hold up my hand to quiet her. Surprisingly, it works. "Thank you, but we are here for a reason. My girlfriend is sick."

Her face falls as soon as the word "girlfriend" falls from my lips.

"Can I have your autograph?"

What. The. Fuck.

I place both hands on the counter and lean through the window. "Listen, my girlfriend is sick and needs to see a doctor. Do your damn job and get her signed in," I seethe.

She instantly starts tapping on the keyboard in front of her. "I'm sorry," she says before asking for all of Stacy's information. I don't have her insurance info—hell, I don't even know if she has any. Instead, I hand over my Amex—it doesn't matter what it costs. I just need her better. "Hand me that." I point to a piece of paper sitting beside her. I scrawl out my name with "thank you for your help," and give it back to her.

She beams, my tirade long forgotten.

I don't even get to sit down before they are calling Stacy back to a room.

"We're good, man. Thanks," I say to Gavin. He nods and heads back to the bus. Stacy gives me a look, daring me to carry her. I don't want to embarrass her, so I place my hand on the small of her back and walk with her into the exam room.

"Hi, Stacy. I'm Todd. What's going on with you today?"

Todd? That's not exactly professional. I watch while "Todd" types a few things on his laptop as Stacy starts to speak.

"I. . . ."

I place my hand on her arm. "She just started feeling bad earlier today." She nods her agreement. "She's got a bad sore throat, headache, body aches and I think she might have a fever."

Stacy, who is sitting on the exam table, leans in to me where I stand right beside her.

"Have you taken anything?"

"She had three Advil about fifteen minutes ago. That's all?" I ask Stacy.

She nods.

"Okay, let me take your vitals and then we'll swab your throat. The doctor will be in to see you after," Todd says.

Doctor? What the hell? I thought he was the doctor?

"Male nurse." He smirks.

Shit. I must have said that out loud.

The room is quiet as he takes her vitals. When it's time for him to swab her throat, she squeezes my hand tight. I know how she feels; I hate that shit.

"This takes about five minutes to run. The doctor will be in with the results," Todd tells us then leaves the room.

"At least he didn't ask for an autograph."

Stacy smiles.

"Can I do anything?" I know there is really nothing I can do for her, but it kills me to see her not feeling well.

She doesn't answer, just leans back against my chest. I stand there by the table and wrap my arms around her, trying to comfort her any way I can. This is new to me—taking care of someone, caring that they're ill. I know it's a sore throat, and after some meds and a few days of rest she'll be good to go, but I want to take that from her. It's a feeling that I couldn't explain if I tried. I don't ever want to see her less than happy, without that blinding smile on her face.

I rub slow, lazy circles on her back. That's how the doctor finds us.

"Hi, Stacy, I'm Doctor Gilbert. Looks like your throat culture came back positive for strep throat. Let's take a look." He stands to look in her throat and feel around on her neck. "Any other symptoms?" he asks as he checks her ears.

Stacy shakes her head.

"Are you allergic to any medications?"

"No," she rasps.

"Great. I'm going to put you on a seven-day regimen. Make sure you take them all. If you're not feeling better in a couple of days, come back to us or see your primary care," he says, never taking his eyes off his computer screen. "Which pharmacy do you use?"

"We're from out of town. Can you just write it and we'll find one close by that's still open? If that's even possible."

"Sure, we can also fill it here. Although, our prices are a little higher as we don't have the volume the retailers do," he explains.

"Fill it."

"All right then. Give us about ten minutes and we'll have it ready for you. You're welcome to wait here or in the waiting room."

"I gave the receptionist my card. Have her charge the visit and the medicine."

"Sure thing. I'll send her in with everything as soon as it's ready. Feel better, Stacy," he says over his shoulder as he leaves the room.

"I don't want to expose Logan and the baby more than I already have," she says, holding her throat.

Shit. I didn't even think about that. I pull my phone out of my pocket and call Kacen.

I explain what's going on. "Can you have Logan pack us a bag? I'm going to just call a cab and get a hotel room. We don't want to risk it with Logan and the baby."

He agrees and I'm ending my call just as the receptionist comes into the room.

"Here's your receipt and your card, Mr. Hampton. The prescription is in the bag."

"Thank you," I say, turning to give all of my attention to Stacy. This girl didn't even acknowledge her. "You ready to get home and get some rest, sweets?"

"Yes." She winces.

"Don't talk. Text me if you have to, but don't talk."

"Do you all have cough drops and Advil here too?" I ask the nosy fucking receptionist, who is still standing there watching us.

"Yeah, right this way. We have our own miniature pharmacy."

After I grab everything I think she might need—and most of it I'm sure she won't—we make our way outside. Gavin hands me a bag and points to the cab. "Logan got you a room, the cabbie knows where he's going. The reservation is under Stacy Hampton." He smirks.

"Thank you." She winces again, holding her throat.

"Don't talk," I scold her. "Thanks, man. I'll call you all tomorrow." I reach for the bag with one hand and Stacy with the other. "Let's get you to bed."

CHAPTER 32

THE SUN HITS MY FACE and I groan. Cole quickly hops out of bed and pulls the blinds.

"Sorry, sweets. I didn't think about closing them last night when we got in."

"Thank you," I croak. Gah! My throat is killing me.

Cole climbs back into bed and snuggles under the covers. He pulls me to him. "Don't talk. You don't have to thank me. I want to take care of you." He places a feather-soft kiss against my temple. "Are you hungry?"

I shake my head.

"Okay, but you need to at least be drinking something. I'm going to call downstairs. You want coffee?"

Another shake of my head. Coffee doesn't sound good to me.

"How about some hot chocolate?"

Again, I shake my head. Reaching over, I grab my cell phone from the nightstand and quickly type out a message.

Me: *Milkshake*

"Milkshake. Why didn't I think of that?" he asks. "Flavor?"

I type out another text.

Me: *Vanilla*

"Anything else sound good to you?"

Me: *No, thank you.*

"I'm going to call downstairs and order it, and then I'll get your medicine." He reaches for the phone on the nightstand and orders himself some breakfast and me a milkshake.

Once he's finished, he pulls me back into his chest and I snuggle up to him. I hate being sick, but it's nice to have this, to have someone who is there to help. Not that I'm not capable of taking care of myself, but it's the thought that he wants to. That he hasn't left my side.

"I need to get your medicine," he finally says, releasing his hold on me.

I move into a sitting position and watch as he pulls on his jeans, then gathers my medication. He pulls a bottle of water from the mini fridge and hands everything to me.

"This one"—he points to a horse pill that will be hell on my throat—"is your antibiotic. The other three are Advil for pain."

I take them from him and swallow them one at a time. I'll be glad when they kick in. I hate this. We were supposed to have three days together to just hang out, and here he is taking care of me. I feel guilty.

Room service arrives not long after and the milkshake feels and tastes like heaven. Cole dives into his breakfast, sitting beside me in the bed.

"You want to try some eggs?"

I grab my phone and send him a text.

Me: *No, but thank you.*

He reads his message and continues eating. Once he's finished, he sets his plate on the floor and rolls over to face me.

Picking up my phone, I send him another text.

Me: *You don't have to stay with me today.*

I watch as he reads it.

"Where else would I be?"

Me: *Call the guys. Go have some fun. This is your time off.*

"You're right, it is. I'm also spending it just as I would have, even if you weren't sick—with you." He taps the end of my nose. "I cherish this alone time that I get with you. We're usually on a crowded bus, so this"—he waves his hand around the room—"is exactly where I want to be."

Me: *What if I get you sick?*

"Then I do. I don't have to sing backup. The guys can cover me, and I can play the guitar without talking. Besides, you're being treated, so it's a chance I'm willing to take."

Sweet Cole is still going strong. I still see his cocky side, but when it matters, when it's important, he never lets me down.

Me: *Watch a movie with me?*

He hands me the remote. "Your choice."

Me: *I don't care what we watch. I'll just fall asleep*

He chuckles as he reads my message. "Okay, sweets, come here." He holds out his arm, and I slide closer and rest my head against his chest. His fingers automatically begin to run through my hair. He scrolls through the stations until he lands on some show about drag racing.

I don't bother to even pretend that I'm paying attention; I close my eyes and let the steady beat of his heart lull me to sleep.

I wake up to Cole talking on the phone.

"Yeah, she's good. She's been sleeping all day."

A pause and then, "Will do." He ends the call.

"Hey." My voice is raspy, but I feel a little better than earlier.

"Hey, sweets, you feeling any better?"

"Yeah." My stomach growls.

"How about some soup? Maybe a grilled cheese?"

"That sounds pretty amazing, actually," I say, holding my throat.

Cole smiles and makes the call then brings me my medicine. "I brought more Advil, every six hours for pain," he explains.

"What time is it?" I ask after taking a drink of the ice-cold water he handed me.

"It's after five."

"I'm sorry I slept all day. You should have called the guys."

He rests his hands on my shoulders. "Stop. This is where I want to be. I got to hold you all day. What's better than that?" He shrugs as if he really doesn't know what would be a better way to spend his day.

I don't bother to argue with him, just take my medicine and drink the entire bottle of water. "I need a shower."

"How about a bath? You can soak until our food gets here. They said forty-five minutes since it's the dinner rush. Sound good?"

"Sounds perfect."

Reaching out, he offers me his hand. I take it, allowing him to help me up from the bed. My body aches.

Once in the bathroom, Cole turns the water on while I brush my teeth. That alone makes me feel human again.

"There's a new toothbrush for you to start using after you've been fever-free for twenty-four hours. I picked one up the other night at the urgent care."

"What made you think of that?"

"Chloe. Mia had strep a while back. When I called to see if she needed anything before I stopped by, she said she needed a new toothbrush for Mia. I looked it up online while you were sleeping to see if there was a suggested time frame." He tests the water temperature. "It's ready for you. Sorry we don't have any bubbles."

"Bubbles not required," I rasp. I finish stripping out of my clothes before joining him beside the tub. Resting my hand on his arm, I hold on as I step into the hot water. Both legs in, I sink down into the warmth. "Will you get in with me?" I ask as he turns to leave.

"I ordered food."

"You said yourself that it will be a while before they get here. Please." I think it's my pathetic voice combined with the pouty lip that causes him to cave.

"Naked time with my girl." He smirks.

I watch unashamed as he slowly strips out of his jeans and boxer briefs.

"Don't look at me like that, sweets."

"Like what?"

"Like you want to devour me." He points to his hard length. "This is what happens when you do that. You're sick, so there is no action happening."

He leaves no room for debate. I know that as long as I still feel like I do and sound like I do, there will be no sexy time with my man.

Cole steps into the tub and settles in behind me, his legs surrounding mine. "Lie back," he says, his voice soft.

I do as he asks and rest my head on his shoulder. He grabs a washcloth that he must have lain on the side of the tub and dunks it into the water. Gently, he runs it over my body.

"Your skin is so soft," he murmurs.

"Mmmm."

It's not until I feel his hands on my breasts that I realize he's lost the washcloth. He uses his hands to cup water and release it over my chest before running them over my breasts and down my stomach. I may be sick, but having his hands on me is a spark that will always find a flame.

Trailing kisses down my neck, his hands continue their path. "You okay with this, sweets?"

"Don't stop," I pant.

He doesn't until those long, slender fingers of his find my center. "Fuck," he hisses.

I grip onto his thighs and hold on for the ride as he slowly works me over until I fall over the edge.

We're both breathing heavily. I can feel his every breath, can see mine as my chest rapidly rises and falls.

"I can't get enough of you."

Turning my head, I place a kiss on his chest.

"Every fucking second that I spend with you beats the one before it. I look forward to those seconds, every damn one of them. I miss you when you're not in my arms. I long to kiss you, to touch you, and to show you how much you mean to me."

I'm glad he's sitting behind me because I couldn't stop the tears if I tried. Somehow, he's found a way into my heart and is expressing everything that's there, right beside the big neon sign with his name on it.

He wraps both arms around my chest and hugs me close. "I should get out and get dried off. The food should be here soon." He kisses my cheek and climbs out of the tub.

I wait until he leaves the room before I climb out on shaking legs. I release the drain on the tub and hop in the shower to wash my hair. It gives me the time I need to get my emotions in check before facing him again.

This damn strep throat kept me from kissing the hell out of him. I wanted to tell him that he has all of me, that I've fallen in love with him, but I refuse to do that if I can't kiss him. If I can't follow my declaration with actions to show him what he means to me.

My sweet Cole.

CHAPTER 33

WE LEAVE OHIO TODAY AND head for Indiana. It's been three days of illness, laughs, hugs, cuddling and "sexy times," as my girl likes to call them. I love what I do; music is a part of me. It's just that Stacy . . . well, she's my heart. I can't live without her. I'm not ready to leave this hotel room, this bubble we've been in for the past three days. I want to stay here, wrapped up in us.

"Okay, I think I've got everything."

I watch as she walks around the room, making sure we won't be leaving anything behind. It's very . . . domestic, and I'm digging it.

"Did you get your medicine?" I ask. I know she's feeling better, but the doctor said she had to take them all. I won't let her forget. I don't want to see her sick again, at least not any time soon. Breaks my fucking heart.

"Got it." She looks in her purse just to make sure she really does have it.

"Tristan just sent me a text saying they're here. The bus is parked in the back lot. It's our best bet to avoid the crowds."

"I still can't believe people have been hanging around here since we checked in just to get a glimpse of us."

"Welcome to my world."

"It's kind of my world now too, you know?"

"You're damn right it is." I pull her into a kiss. She finally let me kiss her yesterday. Fuck you, strep throat!

"Yeah, I mean, I'm the band's assistant to the assistant, or whatever you want to call me."

No, you're mine. "You're more than that," I correct her as I kiss her again.

"Hmmm, you're right. I'm the lead singer's wife's best friend."

She's baiting me. That's fine—I'll tell her a thousand times a day, if that's what it takes.

"You're that too, but there's still more. The most important."

"Let's see." She taps her index finger against her chin. "You're right! I completely forgot about Tristan, Gavin and Kacen. Those guys are like brothers to me."

What? She brings my boys into this before me? "You're mine," I growl before crashing my lips against hers. Thankfully, my cell beeps, reminding me that we need to go.

"That's Tristan. We should head out." I kiss her one more time. Our privacy is gone again, at least for the next four weeks. After that, I'm locking us both in my place for a week, maybe longer. I don't know that I'll ever be okay with sharing her.

She steps back, but I grab her and pull her close again. "I need to hear you say it, sweets."

Smiling up at me, she crooks her finger, beckoning me closer. I bend down until her lips are next to my ear. "There's this guy. His name is Cole Hampton, and he's this big-time rock star, but it's more than that. He makes my heart skip a beat every time he tells me I'm his."

I crush her to my chest. "Always," I breathe against her neck.

My phone goes off again. Fucking Tristan. I'm having a moment with my girl.

"Sweets, we have to go."

"I know. If my boyfriend, Cole, finds me with you, he's going to be pissed."

I smack her ass and she runs toward the door, laughing.

"Come on, slow poke, Tristan's waiting."

When we walk on the bus, they all stop and stare at us. This is the first time we've seen them during the break.

"How are you feeling?" Logan asks Stacy.

"So much better. I'm no longer contagious, I've been fever-free for over forty-eight hours, and I'm still taking my medicine." She crouches down in front of Logan, who is sitting on the couch. "How's this little guy? You been feeling okay? I didn't get you sick, did I?"

Logan laughs. "No, I feel great. This one,"—she pats her ever-growing belly—"he likes to pretend he's playing soccer, and there really isn't that much room."

"How long, eight weeks left?" Stacy asks.

"Yep. I had a checkup yesterday. We actually went to this 'Mommy and Me' place, and I got to have a 4-D ultrasound. You have to see these pictures." She goes to stand, but Tristan scolds her.

"Don't move, woman, I got this." He pulls the pictures from the clip off the refrigerator and hands them to Stacy.

"So, you ready for one of those?" Tristan asks, pointing to the pictures the girls and Kace are now gushing over.

Am I? "Someday," I reply, brushing him off. I've never given it much thought until now. I like kids, and Mia is a ball to be around. I've never thought about being with one woman long enough to want my own, but standing here, watching Stacy smile with Logan as they look at the pictures, I can see it. I can see her growing round with our baby. The thought doesn't scare me; a year ago, it would have.

"She good?" he asks, nodding toward Stacy.

I clap him on the shoulder. "Yeah, man. She's good." Better than good—she's fucking amazing.

"Now that we're all here, the label is putting together an after-party. It's scheduled right after the show in two weeks. They would like for all of us to attend," Gavin explains.

"I guess we've been lucky up to this point. This is the first time they've summoned us," Kacen comments.

"I thought we were going to get lucky," Tristan adds.

"Is this a bad thing?" Logan asks.

"Not really, it's just a fucking dog and pony show. The last thing any of us want to do is schmooze after putting on a show," Kacen explains.

"Girls' night," Stacy says, high-fiving Logan.

"Oh no, sweets. 'All of us' includes the two of you." I hold a hand out to help her up, and she immediately tucks into my side. I fucking love that shit. Love that she knows that's where I want her.

"But we're not part of the band," Logan chimes in.

"Baby, you're my wife. Of course you are." Kacen kisses her.

"And you." Stacy lifts her head to look at me. "You're mine, remember?" I say, just for her ears only.

She grins. "I might be able to get away from my boyfriend, but he gets jealous easily, so we'll have to be covert about it."

I kiss her.

What the hell else am I going to do with her? She gets me, yet she's still mine.

"Ugh, I have nothing party-worthy that fits. Do we have to go?" Logan whines.

"Yes, baby, I want you there. You look beautiful in anything. Besides, it's two weeks from now, which gives you two time to find something new," Kacen croons.

"Something sexy," I whisper in Stacy's ear.

"I'll let them know that we're in," Gavin announces.

"Do we have a choice?" Tristan fires back.

"No, but it's nice to make them think we're playing the game. Because that's exactly what this is," Gavin replies.

"Fucking Wilson," I mumble. The CEO of Stone Records is a dick. He knows we hate this shit, especially after a show, but he doesn't care. It would be different if the party was for the band, because we could come straight from the show, but it's the label's shindig. We have to appear "presentable"—straight from the dick's mouth.

On the bright side, my girl gets to buy a sexy dress, and this time, she'll be going home with me at the end of the night. She makes everything better.

CHAPTER 34

Stacy

TWO MORE WEEKS AND WE'LL be back home. It's been exhausting being on the road, and I'm so ready to sleep in my own bed. That is until I remember that Cole won't be in it. We've managed for both of us to sleep in either his or my bunk every night since we agreed to take this thing between us to another level. Cole insisted that there was no way in hell I was sleeping without him, so we make it work. I was reluctant at first, but I can admit that I would rather be squished in that bunk with him than sleep without him. Surprisingly, it's not all that bad. I snuggle in close and he keeps his arms around me. That's how we both like it.

We haven't talked about how things will be with us when we get home. There's a part of me that's still afraid that the shine of a new relationship will wear off and we'll drift apart. Then I see the way he looks at me and I know I'm being crazy. Cole Hampton doesn't do anything he doesn't want to do, and he *wants* to be with me. I believe that. He's made it a point to assure me each and every day.

Tonight's the after-party. Logan and I went shopping in every city we hit these past two weeks, finally settling on something while in Arkansas. Now we're in Iowa. Logan found a dress that makes her look like a sexy mamma; Kacen is going to shit himself when he sees her. I, on the other hand, went with your basic little black dress with fuck-me heels. I was trying to spend wisely, and I can use a little black dress again. I'm not married to a rock star. I do make decent money, but I'm not sure if my job with the band extends to when the tour is over, so I've been banking as much of it as I can just in case.

The six of us were going to have to get ready on the bus, since we can't get a room tonight. The guys agreed to get ready in their room backstage and give us girls the tiny bathroom on the bus. I think they got the better deal for sure.

The guys have a show tomorrow night in Missouri, which Cole says is a good thing. We stop in, make an appearance at the party, and use the tour schedule as an excuse to cut out early. It's a seven-hour drive to our next location, so it will be wheels up as soon as we make it back to the bus.

Logan and I are in our assigned seats—side-stage. The crowd tonight is loving our boys, who went back out and played three songs over what the set usually is.

"They're stalling!" Logan shouts over the sound of what we hope is the last song of the night.

I throw my head back and laugh. "I think you might be right. Is this guy really that much of a pain in the ass to be around?"

"Honestly, I don't know. He came to the wedding and we briefly said hello. Other than that, I've had no interaction with him. They all say he's a jerk. I think that's part of the reason Gavin is learning as much on the business side as he can. They're all starting to want more than what the label can give them."

I reach over and rub her belly. "Like this little guy?"

Her face radiates happiness. "Yeah, I mean, Cole is the only one who's settled down"—she bumps her shoulder into mine—"but I think the others want it too. It's just a feeling I have."

"Maybe. I've not seen them sleeping around and partying it up. That's kind of what I expected from all three of them," I confess.

"I have to admit, I kind of did too. But I know they're good guys. I think they sleep around because they can and because there hasn't been any one to hold their interest. Look at Cole."

"You're just as surprised about that one as I am. He was relentless."

"They're all that way. Once they set their mind to something, it consumes them."

"I've only seen Cole, and Kacen with you, but they've both been persistent at getting the girl. You think Gavin and Tristan will be the same way?"

"I do. They are all a lot alike. They want what they want and never waver from that. It's going to be fun watching it happen. Trust me, I got to do it with you."

"Ha ha. Well, I got to watch it with you and I agree; it's going to be rather entertaining."

Kacen tells the crowd good night, and this time it's real. I keep my eyes on Cole as he hands off his guitar and makes his way to me. He's done this after every single show. Even before we were official, he always heads straight for me.

Makes a girl get all emotional and shit.

I stand to greet him and he immediately engulfs me in his arms. "I missed you," he says against my neck.

"I've been right here all night."

"No, you've been in that chair all night. I wanted you here." He pulls me closer as if trying to explain.

"I don't think you could have played your guitar with me in your arms."

"You doubt me, woman?"

"No, I would never do that." I laugh.

"Let's go, you. I'll walk you to the bus."

"You guys have to get ready too. All we really have to do is change our clothes and freshen our makeup. The guards will be with us."

"I don't like it."

"You and me both," Kacen chimes in.

"Seriously, it's going to be fine. They paparazzi already have a ton of pictures of us, what's a few more? Besides, we made an effort tonight," Logan states.

"Right? We should probably pose for them," I add. I know it's driving the guys crazy. They worry about the paparazzi and the attention that this lifestyle gets will scare us away.

"They go straight to the bus," Cole tells the guards who are standing just behind us.

"Yes, sir." They both nod with their serious faces in understanding.

I appreciate them, but I would hate to have their jobs.

"Be careful. Don't go anywhere without one of the guards," Cole warns.

"Got it. Now, go shower, you're all sweaty."

"You like me all sweaty." He leans in like he's going to wipe is hair on me.

"Watch it, Hampton! You mess me up, you'll be going to this party by yourself."

"Noooo, I need you there. You'll make it bearable." Bending down, he lightly presses his lips to mine. "I'll see you soon, sweets."

He really has no idea the effect he has on me.

"Ready?" Logan asks.

"Yes." I link my arm through hers. Flanked by the guards who have been assigned to us for the tour, we make our way back to the bus.

It doesn't take us long to get ready. We change into our dresses and touch up our makeup. Fluff the hair and we are good to go.

"Ugh, I feel like a whale," Logan whines.

"Seriously? You look hot. Kacen is going to swallow his damn tongue when he sees you. You're pregnant and glowing. Trust me."

"Let's get this over with. Did you decide if you're wearing a sweater?"

"Yeah, I think I am. There's not much to this dress and it's a little chilly."

"My hormones can't decide if I'm hot or cold. I'm going to grab one just in case."

We grab our bags and step off the bus. Our guards are standing by the door waiting for us. There is also a man decked out in a suit, hair slicked back.

"Ah, who do we have here?" he asks.

One of the guards places his arm out in front of us, as if to shield us from him.

"Come on now, you don't really think I would hurt these two lovely ladies now, do you? I'm looking for the band."

"Not here," our other guard says.

I realize that they've been with us this whole time and I don't even know their names. They rarely speak to us, except "this way," or "wait"—things like that. After this incident, though, I will learn their names. They put their lives on the line for us. Not that we've had any issue up to this point, but it only takes once. Suit guy creeps me out, so I'm grateful they're here.

"I find it hard to believe they would leave these beauties. Mrs. Warren, nice to see you again."

Logan stiffens beside me, but she doesn't respond to him.

Both guards, who are mountains of men, step between us and cross their arms over their chests. "Guys aren't here, move along."

Suit guy chuckles. "See you soon, ladies." He smirks and walks off.

The guards don't move until he's out of sight.

"Let's get you to the party," the one standing in front of me says. He throws an arm over my shoulder and we begin walking to the SUV.

"Logan?"

"She's right behind us," he answers. He's all business, and I make a mental note to thank Cole for insisting that I also have a guard.

Once we're safely in the car and on the road, I reach over and grab Logan's hand. "Did you know that guy?"

"He looks familiar, but I can't place him. I've met so many people since I've been with the band, it's hard to tell. He obviously knows me, or at least knows who I am."

"You guys recognize him?" I ask the guards.

"No, ma'am," Logan's replies.

"We owe you both an apology. You've been by our sides this entire tour and we don't even know your names."

"It's supposed to be like that, ma'am."

"Why?" Logan asks.

"When we get personal with clients, attachments are made. Protecting you becomes personal and we might not react with a clear head," my guy replies.

"But you know us," I counter.

"Yes, ma'am, we do. It's our job to study your patterns and actions. It's what we need to do to protect you. That part is personal, but we keep our lives to ourselves. Helps with personal detachment."

"Must be lonely," Logan muses.

"No, ma'am. We do this for our families back home," her guy replies.

"He was creepy, for sure. I mean, I didn't get serial-killer vibes, but creepy, you know?" Logan says.

"Yeah, he was creepy all right." I think about the incident and then I think about the guys finding out. "Nothing happened, and I never felt like we were in danger, but I can only guess that the guys are going to freak."

"Yeah." She sighs. "Kacen is protective enough."

"I don't suppose we could not tell them?"

My guard grunts. I guess that's a no.

The remainder of the ride is short and quiet. I'm dreading telling the guys, knowing they will surely blow this out of proportion. We were never in danger; the guy was just a creep.

Our guards escort us into the building. My eyes search the room, looking for the Soul Serenade boys.

"They're on their way. About two minutes out," my guard tells us.

Logan and I stand behind them, backs to the wall. I can only imagine how ridiculous we look.

"What the fuck happened?" I hear Kacen's booming voice.

Here we go.

Cole's long strides carry him directly to me. Reaching out, he grabs my hand and pulls me in to him. "What happened?" He's holding on tight to his anger. I'm impressed, actually.

"Nothing, some creepy guy in a suit with slicked back hair was waiting outside the bus. He said he was looking for the band, and he knew who Logan was, but she didn't recognize him," I'm quick to explain. Who knows how long until the fuse is lit.

"Did he touch you? Logan?" he grits out.

I resist the urge to roll my eyes. Instead, I place my hands on either side of his face, capturing his full attention. "No. I told you what happened. They"—I motion with my head to our guards, who have stepped back a few feet. Neither has said a word, letting the guys talk to us first—"are just being cautious. Doing the job you hired them to do. We're both fine. Nothing inappropriate was even said. The guy just gave us the creeps."

Cole buries his face in my neck. Wrapping my arms around his waist, I hold on tight.

Finally, lifting his head, he seeks out the guard assigned to me. Keeping me close, he offers him his hand. "Thank you."

"Sir." He nods.

No other words are spoken. Cole wraps himself around me and again buries his face in my neck.

I hear Kacen thank the guards as well and tell them they can take a break. "We're going to go find a table," he tells us.

"Yeah, man. I think we're going to go get some air. We'll be right back," Cole informs him.

Cole leads us across the room and down a hall, a set of French doors at the end. Pulling on the handle, the door opens and he ushers us out onto the small balcony.

I walk toward the edge and he pulls me back. "I just need to hold you for a minute."

I relax into his embrace, soaking up his warmth.

"We got a message from Zack and Chad. They're required to report everything to us. The message said, 'We had an issue with a man outside the bus, but it's handled and the girls are safe.'" He kisses the top of my head. "I've never felt that kind of fear, Stacy. The message said you were safe, but it didn't tell me if you were hurt."

"I'm fine. The guy just gave us the creeps. He didn't touch us, didn't say anything out of line. He was just . . . odd," I try to soothe him.

"I get that, I do. When I got the message, I didn't know." Pulling back, he places my hands over his heart and then brings his to gently caress each cheek. "You feel that?"

I assume he means the rapid beat of his heart against my hand. I nod.

"That's you. You're inside me." He kissed my forehead. Pulling back just far enough where his eyes can lock with mine, he watches me. I don't know how long we stand there, but it seems like hours before he finally says, "I love you."

Butterflies dance in my stomach as his words sink in.

He loves me!

I stand on tiptoes so our lips are barely touching. "I love you, too." I kiss his lips, softly.

"Yeah?" he asks, hopeful.

"Yeah, I was afraid to tell you. I didn't want to scare you away."

"Baby, nothing could scare me away from you." He kisses me once more, his soft yet firm lips caressing mine.

"We better get back in there. You're here to make an appearance."

"I just need another minute," he says, holding me against his chest. "I don't ever want to feel like that again. Like my entire world is crashing around me. I need to put your ass in a bubble."

"Come on, crazy man, let's get moving. The faster we get this over with the sooner we can get back to the bus."

His eyes light up. "I love you," he says again, as runs his thumb across my lips.

I'm sure my lip-gloss is long gone.

Inside, we find the rest of our crew at a table. Logan gives me a smile, letting me know that she was also able to calm her man down.

My man.

He loves me.

"You good, man?" Gavin asks Cole.

He has his arm slung over my shoulders. Leaning in, he kisses my temple. "Never better." The creepy man long since forgotten.

"Glad you could make it," a strange voice says from the end of the table.

Looking up, I see him. Creepy guy.

"Ladies, it's nice to see you again," he continues.

Cole whips his head around to look at me, then Logan. I nod, letting him know this is the guy.

"Wilson, what the fuck? What are you doing hanging around outside our bus?" Cole seethes.

Creepy guy—Wilson—throws his head back and laughs. "Why, looking for you, of course. I see your flavor of the week told you I stopped by."

Cole tries to stand, but I hold tight to his arm. "Let it go," I plead.

"What do you want, Wilson?" Kacen asks.

"Just wanted to make sure you all were going to show up. I'm not used to this . . . domesticated version of the band." He sweeps his eyes over Logan and stops on me, blatantly staring at my chest until Cole growls.

I pull my sweater closed to block his view. It's not like the girls are hanging out but, this guy is not getting a peek of anything.

"Watch it," Cole warns.

Wilson holds his glass of amber liquid in the air as a toast and walks away.

"I hate that prick," Gavin seethes.

I look over and see that his knuckles are turning white as he grips the beer bottle in his hand.

"Who is that?" Logan asks.

"*That* is Fuck-stick Wilson, the CEO of Stone Records," Tristan explains.

"He's the one?" Kacen confirms with Logan.

"That's him, but he didn't do anything. He wasn't inappropriate or anything. We just got a weird vibe from him," Logan tells him once again.

These men are fiercely protective.

"Good show tonight," Bobby Jones, the band's manager, says as he approaches the table.

"Thanks, man." Cole shakes his hand, as do the other guys.

"Ladies, you look lovely as ever," he comments.

Logan and I both mumble an embarrassed "Thank you."

"So, there are a few people Wilson wants me to introduce you to. Once we get that over with, you all are free to go. I know you have a long night of driving ahead of you."

"Whose ass are we kissing this time?" Gavin asks.

Bobby chuckles. "Wilson is trying to sign a new band. Trying to convince them to leave their current label. He just wants to brag that he signed the hottest rock band out there."

Tristan finishes off his beer. "Let's get this over with and get the hell out of here." He types out a text then shoves his phone back in his pocket.

"The guards are outside," Cole says.

I place my hand on his leg. "We'll be fine. We are in a room full of crowded people, and you already know who it was. He wasn't there to hurt us, Cole. He's just an ass," I scold him.

Leaning in, he kisses the corner of my mouth, trailing his lips across my cheek until they meet my ear. He nips at my lobe before he whispers, "I'll be right back, sweets. I love you."

I beam at him.

The guys reluctantly leave us to schmooze. "What was that?" Logan asks, wearing a grin.

"What was what?"

"That?" She points her finger at my face and makes a circle. "What did I miss?"

I shrug. "He told me he loves me." I act like it's not a big deal when all I want to do is scream and jump around the room.

"Stacy! I told you! EEEPP! I'm so excited."

"I'm going to go grab us a drink. Water?"

"Yes, please. Hopefully, the guys will be back soon and we can get out of here." She rubs her pregnant belly. "This one has worn me out today."

I reach over and rub her baby bump. "Be right back."

On the way to the bar, I see the sign for restrooms and decide to stop in and touch up my lip-gloss.

I take in my flushed face, the smile that is permanently etched there, and my heart feels full. Never would I have thought I would be here. That Cole would settle down with me. Not that we're settled really, but he loves me, so that's something. I quickly run my tube of lip-gloss over my lips, drop the tube back in my bag, and head back to the bar. As soon as I walk out the door, his voice stops me.

"Cole seems enamored," Wilson says.

Ugh! What is with *this guy?* "Logan's waiting on me. It was good to see you," I say politely and turn to walk away.

"I wasn't done talking to you, bitch," he seethes as he reaches out and grabs my arm, yanking me back toward him.

"Take your hands off me."

"Feisty one. Is that why he's stuck with you?" He tightens his grip on my arm. Leaning in close, he runs his nose up my cheek.

"Don't touch me." I turn my head, but he squeezes my arm even tighter.

"Do you fight him? Huh? Is that what it is?"

I clench my teeth shut, willing him to let me go.

"You see, I used to make money from them—on the side, of course. Those boys like to play. I have some paps in my back pocket, on the payroll if you will. They take the pictures and I sell them. It's a win-win. That is until spoiled princesses like yourself and your friend fuck it all up. Why is that? What is it you have that the others don't?"

He runs his fingers up my thigh. I move my leg to try and kick him, but it just pisses him off. His grip on my arms gets even tighter.

"Stop fucking fighting me. Is it your pussy? Is it made of gold? Maybe it's the taste?" Again, he trails his hand up my thigh, further this time. "They don't party anymore, they don't fuck random women. You know what that means? That means you are taking money from my pocket. I don't fucking take kindly to that. Especially not from whores."

Tears fall from my eyes. "Please, stop," I beg him.

He leans in close and licks my cheek, the smell of liquor almost knocking me over. "I want a taste. I need to see what the hype is all about."

"No!" I scream. He pushes me against the wall, holding my arms in the air. I try again to kick him, but he just moves his big body in close, blocking me. Just, when I've come to accept my fate, that this man is about to violate me, I hear voices.

"Fuck!" He looks down the hall then back at me. "Listen, you fucking whore, this didn't happen. If I hear you breathe one word, I'll ruin your sugar daddy. Soul Serenade will never play another venue." He grinds his crotch against me. "Fucking answer me," he slurs.

"Yes, please, yes. I understand. Just let me go." The tears are coming full force.

He pushes off the wall, giving me one last menacing look before he saunters down the hall as if nothing happened.

I scramble to pick up my purse and run back into the bathroom. I check to make sure I'm alone and lock the door. I need a minute to get myself together. My heart is racing, and my entire body is shaking. Grabbing a paper towel, I run it under the warm water and wash where he licked me face. I want a shower, to wash away the feeling of his hands on me.

I splash cold water on my face and try to get myself under control. What the hell am I going to do? I've been gone too long for Logan not to know something's up. Shit, the guys could even be back by now. Reaching into my purse, I see that Logan texted me.

***Logan:** You okay?*

Shit! My hands shake as I type back a message.

***Me:** Yeah, just not feeling well all of a sudden. In the restroom. Be back in a minute.*

I can't tell them. I can't be the reason that Cole and the band lose everything. Nothing happened, really. He stopped. I swallow hard at the thought of what could have happened.

I need to just let it go. I can't tell him—Cole will kill him. If Wilson doesn't follow through on his threat, he'll be in jail anyway, so it won't matter.

Deep breath in. I have to do this. I can't let this affect the band. My arms are still aching from where he grabbed me. Pulling up the sleeve of my sweater, I gasp.

Bruises.

I already have dark purple bruises all up and down my arms.

Shit. Shit. Shit. Shit.

I cannot let Cole see this, but how in the fuck am I going to hide them? An all new set of tears burns my eyes. No. I need to pull it together and get out there. The longer I stand here, staring at the evidence, the more suspicious they'll get. Pulling down my sleeves, I wipe my eyes, applying powder to cover the blotchy red spots.

I'm going with the not feeling well; it's not a stretch, since just last month I was ill with strep throat. I'll play it off for a few days and then I will erase it from my mind.

Time to pull up your big-girl panties, Stacy.

CHAPTER 35

COLE

WE'VE BEEN TALKING TO THESE guys a hell of a lot longer than what I thought we would have to. They're pretty cool dudes; I remember Jones having us listen to a demo of them. If it weren't for the fact that my girl is in this same building dressed to kill in that sexy little black dress, I wouldn't mind hanging around to shoot the shit.

Not tonight, though.

Tonight, I have to get my girl. The one I just confessed my love for not ten minutes before I was dragged away from her. Not the most romantic confession, but I couldn't fucking hold it in any longer. I was scared out of my damn mind, not knowing if she was safe.

"All right, well, these guys need to hit the road. Another show tomorrow night," Jones finally says, and I swear I could fucking hug him.

We say our good-byes with the promise to get together and jam sometime and head back to the girls.

Logan is sitting at the table by herself. Looking around, I spot Stacy walking toward us, her face flushed. I immediately break away from the guys and, in just a few long strides, am standing in front of her.

"What's wrong?" I cup her face in my hands.

"I don't feel real well." She leans her forehead against my chest, her arms crossed over her own, tucked in tight against her body.

Smoothing my hand over her shoulders and down her back, I ask, "Are you cold?"

"Yeah. How much longer before we can go?"

"Stacy, are you all right? You were gone forever." Logan and Kacen appear beside us.

"Yeah, I just . . . didn't feel good all of a sudden, so I went to the restroom to splash some water on my face. Just hit," she meekly replies.

"I'm taking her to the bus," I tell them.

"We're coming with you. Gavin and Tristan just left to tell the driver and the crew to get ready to roll out," Kacen explains.

"Let's get you to the bus." My arm goes around her shoulders and she huddles into my side.

I hate this. I hate seeing her not feel well. I have this protective instinct when it comes to her, and my mind doesn't rationalize well. Like now, I just want to get her back to the bus and curl up with her in my arms. I want to make it better, make it go away.

"I'm gonna shower," Stacy says as soon as we step foot on the bus.

"Okay, sweets. You need anything?"

"No, just hoping a shower will help."

I watch her as she gathers clothes and disappears into the small bathroom.

"She's not usually like this. Strep once a year and she's usually good after that. Maybe it's being on the road, and her system is just out of whack?" Logan comments.

"I don't know, but I fucking hate it."

"Baby, let's get you off your feet." Kacen takes her by the hand and leads her to the couch.

"Let's just go to bed," she suggests.

"We can do that. I'll help get you settled, make sure we get on the road, and then I'll join you."

Six months ago, I would have thought Kacen was blinded by love. I would have rolled my eyes laughing at how whipped he sounds. Tonight, I get it. I now know why he's so soft with her. Why he caters to her like she can't do it herself when we all know she can. I now know how it feels to have someone else be a part of you. The other part of your heart. As fucked up as it may sound, I get it. Stacy is that person for me.

Sitting on the couch, I rest my elbows on my knees and bury my face in my hands. Tonight could not be more fucked. I confess that I'm in love with her after I overreact at a situation that is obviously nothing. Then I get pulled away from her when she's all dressed up—for me. When I can finally get away, she's no longer feeling well. I botched the "I love you" and now I can't even make it better. She's sick. Just goes to show you that life is never what you expect. There will always be obstacles to overcome.

As soon as I hear the bathroom door open, I'm on my feet. Stacy emerges with her hair still wet, hanging over her shoulder. She's wearing a pair of those tight things she and Logan are always wearing and my sweatshirt. It's the first time I've seen her in my clothes, and it damn sure won't be the last.

Approaching her, I tug on the hem of the sweatshirt, which swallows her. "I look good on you." I wink at her.

Her too-pale face smiles up at me. "It smells like you." She brings the collar to her nose and sniffs.

I'm hard as a fucking rock and can't do a damn thing about it since she doesn't feel well. I shift to adjust and she notices, her eyes falling to my crotch.

"Cole. . . ." she trails off.

Shit. "I can't help it that you're so goddamn beautiful. He salutes what he likes," I tease her.

"I don't. . . ."

I cup her cheek. "I know, baby. I just want to hold you. He's going to figure it out sooner or later." Yes, my cock has a mind of his own. He needs to learn, though, that she will always come first. It's a new concept for both of us. "Let's go to bed."

With a small nod, she turns toward the bunks. I place my hands on her hips and walk slowly behind her. She slides into the bottom bunk and I climb in behind her, pulling the curtain closed. Curling in a ball, she faces the wall. I slide a hand under the sweatshirt and rest my palm against her smooth skin, then bury my face in her neck, just breathing her in.

"I'm sorry about tonight," I whisper.

Her body stiffens. "What?"

"I botched it. I should have waited for a more romantic time and place to tell you how much I love you." I kiss her neck.

She instantly relaxes.

"I wanted the first time I told you to be special, but I just couldn't . . . In that moment, I needed you to know."

"I wouldn't change it, Cole. It's you. You're confident and cocky, but you're also my sweet Cole. It wasn't botched. It was honest."

I kiss her temple then place my lips next to her ear. "I want to be your lover and your best friend." I nip at her ear.

This gets her attention. Turning her head, she looks at me. "You remember," she whispers.

"Every fucking word you've ever said, sweets," I assure her.

Turning her head back to face the wall, it's quiet until I hear her sniff. "I love you, too."

"Stacy?"

"I'm fine. I just don't feel good, but my heart is full. Full of you, full of us. I need you to know that."

I scoot in as close as I can get to her. "I know, baby. Mine too." I hold her close until we both eventually drift off to sleep.

CHAPTER 36

Stacy

I'VE BEEN AWAKE FOR HOURS. Long enough to know we reached our destination. I've been lying here trying to figure out how I'm going to explain the bruises, or better yet how to hide them.

One thing I do know is that I can't tell him. I can't tell anyone. I will not have the demise of Soul Serenade on my hands. Those four men have worked hard to get where they are, and I'm not going to ruin it for them. Besides, nothing happened. I just need to be more aware of my surroundings, make sure I'm not alone. It's a solid plan. Now if I could just decide on what to do with the bruises.

Cole shifts behind me and I know I'm running out of time. Luckily, it's been cooling off, so I could get away with a long-sleeve T-shirt. I'll make sure it's my Soul Serenade shirt. I can use the "I don't feel well" card and the excuse that I'm cold. I can pull that off.

What I'm really struggling with is Cole. How am I going to keep him from seeing them? I run through the tour schedule in my mind, and luckily, we don't have any breaks where we can get a room for the night. That will help. No way could I get away with staying covered if we had a room to ourselves. He would know without a doubt that I'm hiding something.

Cole's hand that has been under my shirt—well, *his* shirt—all night snakes up toward my chest. "Morning, sweets. How you feeling?" his sleep-laced voices asks as he palms my breast.

Any other day, I would be doing whatever I could in this cramped space to give him more of me, to see and to touch more of him. Not today. Today, I pretend to be sick.

"I'm just feeling blah, I guess. Nothing hurts, just cold," I lie, burrowing into the covers to make it more believable. I'm going to hell for this. I either lie to the man I love, or tell him the truth and ruin what he and his band have busted their asses for. There is no good ending to either solution, so I'm just going to hold onto him. Cherish every touch, every kiss and pray that fuck-stick Wilson doesn't spill. Surely, he's smarter than that, right?

"Can I do anything?"

"I think I just need to rest." Another lie falling from my lips.

"Are you hungry?" He reaches up to the small shelf above and grabs his phone. "I can make you some breakfast."

"You cook?"

He laughs. "I was thinking like a toasted bagel."

"Okay, Mr. Hampton. Dazzle me with your toasting skills."

"Oh, don't you worry."

I roll over slowly to face him. I bite my tongue when I hit my arm on the side of the bus. Shit, that hurts!

"You haven't seen anything until you've seen me spread cream cheese." He winks.

Cocky ass.

"Uh-huh. Let me up, crazy man, I have to pee."

Sweet Cole returns as he kisses my forehead before rolling out of the bunk.

I rush past him and into the small bathroom, locking the door. Once I've handled my business, I push back my sleeves to wash my hands and dark purple bruises cover my arms.

Shit.

I do bruise easily, but these look like I've been beaten. You can see exactly where his fingers were. I swallow the lump in my throat, knowing

I'm lucky he didn't take it further. The look in his eyes said he wanted to. I have never been so grateful for the interruption of voices in my life.

A single tear slides down my cheek as I think about lying to Cole, to Logan and the rest of the guys. I hate Wilson and the position he's put me in. I hate that I really, truly, *finally* believe that what Cole wants is more than just to get his dick wet and that I'm the one who could screw it all up. I avoided him thinking he would use me and here I am being the liar in the relationship.

"You okay in there, sweets?" Cole lightly knocks on the door.

I wipe my face and clear my throat. "Yeah, just washing my hands."

When I make it to the living area, Cole is already eating his bagel. Mine sits on a plate next to him.

"You, okay?"

"Yeah, just moving slow."

"Eat and we can go lie back down. I don't have to be at sound check for a few hours."

"You don't have to wait around with me, Cole. I'm sure you have things to do today. You guys are always busy on show days."

The bagel he's holding stops just before he takes a bite. Slowly, he places it back on the paper plate. That same hand cups my cheek. "You. You are what's important. I don't want to be anywhere but here. I can blow off the radio interview. We've all done it a time or two, claiming other obligations. The only thing I won't do, unless it's an emergency, is bail on the show. The guys depend on me. Please don't take that the wrong way, but it's my job."

"Never. This is your career, Cole. I understand the sacrifices that you have to make."

"And you. As my girlfriend, there will sacrifices that you will have to make as well. Spending the holidays on the road, possibly missed birthdays or anniversaries."

I know all too well about sacrifices. I take a drink of my orange juice, giving myself time to shake off the memories of last night. "Sounds like a long-term thing." I'm baiting him, but I just can't help it. I don't want to push him to talk about the future, but teasing I can do. Besides, the conversation needs to change from talking about sacrifices.

That I'm living.

Leaning in, he kisses me softly. "I love you. That's long-term, sweets," he says, going back to his breakfast.

Be still my heart. Cole Hampton, rocker extraordinaire, is lethal. He should come with a warning label. No wonder Logan fell as hard as she did. I mean, I watched her and Kacen and I could see the connection. Cole and his man bun, his cocky attitude and his words . . . I'm like putty in his hands.

"Where is everyone?" I ask him.

"Gavin and Tristan are sleeping. I assume Kacen and Logan are as well."

"What time is it?"

"Seven."

Damn! My worry has us up early. "I'm sorry I woke you. You should go back to bed."

"Finish your breakfast and we'll go lie down for a few hours." He shoves the last bite—or rather half of his bagel—into his mouth.

I manage to eat one half and slide the other over to him. He finishes it off in a couple of big bites while I throw our trash away. "I'm going to lie down," I tell him.

"I'm going to grab a quick shower before everyone gets up. I'll be there in a minute."

Crawling back into the bottom bunk, I burrow under the covers. It's a dreary day, which is good—it fits my mood. I hear the door to Kacen and Logan's room open. I wish I could talk to her about this, but I don't want to risk her telling Kacen and besides that, she doesn't need the stress. It's not good for her or the baby.

I hear Cole greet them. "Listen, man. Stacy still isn't feeling well. I'm going to skip the radio spot so I can stay with her. I'll be at sound check."

"Need anything?" Kacen asks.

"Nah, just want to be there for her, you know?"

"Cole, thank you," Logan says.

"For?"

"Taking care of her. She deserves someone like you. Fiercely protective and caring all at the same time."

"I love her," is his simple reply.

I can only imagine what Logan's face looks like. I'm sure she's grinning like a damn fool right now.

Cole slowly pulls back the curtain and crawls in next to me. He doesn't say a word as he tucks me in close, my back to his front. There is nothing like his strong arms wrapped around me. He makes it better, makes everything better.

A few hours later, I wake up sweating. Cole and all of his muscles throw off the heat. Not to mention the blanket and his sweatshirt I'm wearing.

"Feeling any better?" His voice startles me.

"How long have you been awake?"

"About an hour or so."

"You've just been watching me sleep?"

"Yeah." He brushes my wild hair from my eyes. "It's suddenly one of my favorite things to do."

"When is sound check?"

"I need to be leaving. I was trying to wait as long as I could to wake you up. Logan and the guys are already there. I told them I would meet them."

"Go! They're waiting on you." I push on him, but he doesn't move.

"You going to be okay here? I can wait until you're ready to come with me."

"Yes, I'll be fine. I'm going to take a shower and just relax. Maybe read a little."

"You think you'll feel like coming to the show?" I can hear the hope in his voice.

"Yes." I kiss his chin. "I have to keep the groupies away from my man."

Leaning over, he captures my lips with his. "Say it again," he breathes.

"I have to keep the groupies away."

"No, the other part." He kisses me again.

"Oh, you mean 'my man'? Yeah, Tristan needs the extra coverage." I can see the fire in his eyes.

"Mine," he declares as he kisses me hard.

His hand snakes under the sweatshirt I'm wearing and that's when I remember—I can't get naked with him, not yet. I need to stop this. "Go,

I have to make myself rock star-girlfriend material."

"You're fucking beautiful right here, right now. I would walk off this bus with you on my arm and be damn fucking honored that it's you."

"I love you, Cole Hampton. Now, go. I'll be here when you get back."

With one last kiss, he's gone. I exhale in relief. Since I can get ready without anyone here, there is less of a chance of them seeing what I'm hiding.

CHAPTER 37

THE CROWDS ON THIS TOUR keep getting better and better. The rush of knowing that thousands of people come out each night just to watch us will never get old. I watch from my spot on the stage as Kacen interacts with the crowd.

"It's fucking hot in here!" he bellows into the microphone as he rips his T-shirt over his head. I throw my head back and laugh as he tosses it out to the crowd. People are diving just to touch a shirt that he wore.

That shit is crazy! I don't think it's something I will ever get used to. Glancing over, I see Logan wearing a grin, her hands protectively on their baby. She knows just like the rest of the world that this is all show. Kacen only has eyes for his wife. He's adamant about the fact and will tell anyone willing to listen.

Stacy is sitting next to Logan, nodding along to the beat that Tristan is now tapping out on his drums. I force myself to take my eyes off her and get my head back in the show.

"Kace, my man, you shouldn't have done that," I say into my mic.

"Here we go," Gavin chimes in.

"It's fucking hot up here, center-stage, C," Kacen replies, and the crowd goes wild.

Gavin and I join Kace center-stage. "Ladies, we need some help," I address the crowd.

"You see, Kace here has all this." Gavin points to Kacen. "But we think you would rather see this." He points to me.

I slide my guitar to my back and lift my shirt. The deafening screams of the ladies fill the arena.

"Or," I say, pulling my shirt, back down, "this." I point to Gavin and he mimics what I just did, pulling up his shirt.

The beat stops. "Hold up, fellas." Tristan grabs his mic and steps down from the drums. "Looks to me like they need to be able to read the full menu before ordering." He stops beside me. "Right, ladies?"

It amazes me the men who toss their women on their shoulders just to get closer to us. If that was me, and it was Stacy, I don't think I could do it. I don't think I could watch her drool and scream over a guy who wasn't me. It's also surprising that a good majority of our fan base is women. Who knew?

Tristan takes his turn and, of course, the crowd goes wild.

"Well, my beautiful wife is the only opinion that matters." Kacen looks to the side-stage area and holds his hand out.

As if they share a brain, Logan slowly stands and walks toward us. He meets her halfway, kissing her before they go any further.

"You all have met my wife, right? Baby, meet this kick-ass crowd we have tonight." Again, the roars fill the arena.

Logan gives a shy wave. "You heard it, ladies. Your options just dwindled down to three," Gavin informs them.

The crowd eats this shit up and gives us time to catch our breath before finishing the show. Suddenly, an idea hits. "Make that two, my man. My girl is backstage," I confess.

I look over at Stacy and she's grinning. No matter what gets thrown at her, at us, she's wearing that smile for me. I decide to push my luck a little and hold my hand out for her, just like Kacen did for Logan.

She shakes her head.

"They want to meet you, sweets," I say into the mic. The crowd lets her know that what I say is true.

She shakes her head again and I can almost read her mind. "Logan's a wife, I'm just a girlfriend." But she's more than that. Someday, I will convince her of the fact.

"Stacy," I say. The microphone picks it up and they start chanting her name.

"Stacy, Stacy, Stacy."

Reluctantly, she stands and takes a hesitant step. That's all I need. I jog to her and wrap my arm around her shoulders. Leaning over, I kiss the top of her head as we join the group center-stage. "Here she is. Babe, meet tonight's crowd."

More cheers and chants of her name flow through the arena.

"Looks like our boy Cole is officially off the market. That leaves these two jokers." Kacen points to Tristan and Gavin.

"Winner gets bragging rights," I say, keeping Stacy tucked into my side.

"Now, let's do this so we can get back to fucking rocking!" Kacen booms into the microphone. "When I point, you need to make some noise. Loudest is the winner, you know the drill," he explains to the crowd.

I drown out the rest of what's going on.

She's all I see.

With my arm still around her shoulders, I guide her to stand in front of me. When I have her where I want her, I place one hand on the small of her back, holding her to me, and the other lifts her chin. I don't speak and neither does she. It wouldn't matter anyway; the noise of the crowd would drown it out. Instead of words, I give her actions. Bending down, I capture her lips with mine. Instantly, her arms wrap around my neck and I allow myself to get lost in her.

Mine.

When I finally pull away from her, I realize the crowd is on fucking fire, cheering and screaming. I look over at Kacen and he's wearing a wide grin.

"Don't stop on our account." My eyes shift to Tristan. He waves over the crowd. "We're enjoying the show."

Stacy immediately buries her face in my chest and I hold her tight. Gavin smirks and hands me a microphone.

"What? You've never seen a man kiss the woman he loves before?"

Thunderous.

The fucking crowd is *thunderous* as they roar with their approval.

I kiss the top of her head, still buried in my chest, before bringing the microphone to my lips. "I'll see you after the show, sweets."

I feel her nod against me, and then she turns on her heel and runs to her seat side-stage. Logan winks as she waddles in the same direction.

Tristan is already behind his drums and starts the beat for our next song. We don't stop again, playing six more songs straight through before calling it a night.

As it's come to be my routine, I hand off my guitar and make strides toward my girl. As soon as I reach her, fucking Wilson shows up from God only knows where. I assumed he would be at the show tonight since he is in town, but I was hoping we didn't have to be graced with his presence.

Stacy looks at him, then at me, then the rest of the guys as we're all gathered in a circle.

"I-I-I have to g-go," she stammers.

"Stacy." I reach for her, but she's too quick. She's already running away from me.

Logan has her hand on my chest before I can move. "Let her go, Cole. They're already with her."

Looking up, I see that her guard has indeed caught up with her.

"I'm heading to the bus. You do what you need to do." Logan motions toward Wilson. "We'll see you guys soon. Let me talk to her."

"I need to go to her." I run my fingers through my sweat-soaked hair. I pull the tie off of my wrist and tie in a knot.

"Let her go, man. This is all new to her. Let Logan talk to her first," Kacen tries to reason.

Clenching my jaw, I nod. I don't fucking like it, but I'm at a loss. Looking over at Wilson, I say, "What the fuck do you want?"

"Now, Cole, is that any way to talk to the man who holds your future."

"Fuck you, our contract is almost up. What do you want?" I seethe.

That fucker laughs. "I just wanted to say congratulations on a great show. That new bit you did with the girls, the crowd loved it. How did you convince her to play along?"

What the fuck? "Did you hit your head? What the hell are you taking about?"

"The girl."

My hands instantly ball into fists at my sides.

I feel a hand on my chest, but I don't know whose it is. "Calm."

Gavin.

"That girl," I grit out, "is mine. You stay the fuck away from her."

He fucking throws his head back as he laughs this time. "She must be sweet, to have your balls in a vise. I wouldn't mind a taste," he boasts.

Motherfucker!

I lunge forward, but all three of my bandmates, my brothers from another mother, stop me. All three of them are holding me back, and it's barely working. I'm insanely fucking pissed off.

"Don't fucking talk about her, don't look at her, don't fucking *breathe* around her," I spit at him, because Gavin and Tristan each have an arm, and Kacen is standing in front of me, hands on my chest, pushing me back.

I'm not moving.

"Is there a problem here?" the security officer asks.

"Yes, he's harassing us," Kacen speaks up.

"I will fucking kill you, do you hear me? You ever come near her and I will fucking *end you!*" I scream at him.

"Sir, you have to calm down," a security guard, who takes Kacen's spot in front of me, says.

"Get him the fuck out of here," I growl.

I don't know what he says to them, but two guards flank Wilson and lead him away. I didn't even get to swing.

"Stacy." That's all I say, and the guys seem to understand.

"I'll take him. You two okay to clear out?" Kacen asks.

"We got it. We'll get there as soon as we can," one of them replies. I'm in too much of a fog to recognize their voice.

I need to get to her.

She ran from me, and then . . . fucking Wilson.

Gavin and Tristan release me and I run. I run through the fans, the roadies, the paparazzi—I run to her.

I don't stop until I reach the bus. I sling open the door and find Stacy and Logan on the coach. Stacy has tears streaming down her cheeks and Logan looks worried.

I immediately drop to my knees in front of her. "Hey, sweets." My voice cracks. She doesn't look at me. My heart is about to beat out of my chest. I take a few deep breaths then try again. "Stacy, can you look at me?" She still doesn't respond. She just cries. Big tears falling from her eyes, each one cracking my fucking heart wide open.

Standing, I lift her in my arms and take her spot on the couch. She immediately buries her face in my neck as a sob breaks free from her chest.

What. The. Fuck?

My mind races with what could cause this kind of reaction from her. I know she wasn't feeling well, but something tells me this is bigger than that.

Keeping one arm around her, holding her to me, the other soothingly strokes her hair. I let her cry, hold her while she falls apart. Logan sits beside me, her hand on Stacy's leg. Kace stands beside Logan with his hand on her shoulder, offering support. None of us says a word; we just let her get it all out. I kiss the top of her head over and over again. Sending up silent prayers that whatever this is, she knows that I'm here, that I want to be nowhere else but where she is.

Her cries soften and she's no longer shaking. Gavin and Tristan came in about fifteen minutes ago. One look at my girl and Tristan told the guards, "No one gets in or out," shut the door, and locked it. They've been leaning against the counter ever since.

"Baby," I whisper. "Please talk to me." I'm pleading, but I don't fucking care. I'm scared out of my mind. "What happened?"

"Oh, my God," she breathes and jumps up from my lap.

I reach out to grab her arm, to stop her, and she flinches while yelping in pain.

What?

I jump to my feet. "I barely touched you," I state the obvious.

"No. No, no, no, no, no," she repeats over and over again.

I know she's not doing drugs; I would notice that. Tears are again flowing, faster than ever, coating her now red and blotchy cheeks. I gently take her hand in mine and pull up the sleeve of her T-shirt.

Bruises.

Fucking dark, black and purple bruises. I drop to my knees and study her arm. Fingerprints. It looks like motherfucking fingerprints on her skin.

Squeezing my eyes closed, I suck in a deep breath. I need to keep my head about me; she's already scared out of her damn mind.

"Baby, what happened?" My voice is so gruff that I barely recognize it.

"I'm sorry, I'm so sorry."

Sorry? "Stacy, I need you to tell me what happened."

"Stacy?" Logan's crying too.

"Stace babe, who did this to you?" Gavin asks.

"I'm sorry." She buries her face in her hands.

Standing, I pick her up again and carry us to the couch on shaking legs. I need to hold her. I need to have her keep me rooted or I might just kill a motherfucker. I still will, as soon as I know she's okay and I find out who put his hands on her.

I pull her as close to me as I can get her, bury my face in her neck, and breathe her in.

"Cole," she sobs.

I have to know who did this. I have to fix it. My girl is broken, and it feels like a knife to the gut.

"Baby, I need you to tell me. Whatever it is, you don't need to be sorry. I just need you to tell me," I beg her.

"We're all here, Stacy. Nothing is going to happen," Logan soothes her.

"I . . . I was trying to protect you. He said he would ruin the band."

Finally! She's talking. Now I just need to keep my cool until she finishes her story.

"Who did, Stacy? Who did this to you?"

"I lied. I'm so sorry I lied. Please, I can't lose you."

That loud noise? That was my heart breaking open for her. For the anguish she's feeling. I feel it too.

"Start at the beginning, beautiful. I'm not going anywhere." I tighten my arms around her to reinforce my words.

"Wilson, he caught me in the hall last night when I went to the bar," she begins her story.

With every word, my anger rises. If she were not a crying mess in my arms, I would have already been out looking for that bastard. He touched her, her soft skin that I've traced with my lips. Her thighs, the ones that hold me tight every fucking time I slide home, deep inside her.

He's a fucking dead man.

The earlier conversation with him after the show now makes sense.

"He said that if I told you, he would end the band. I didn't want to lie to you, I swear, I didn't. Cole, you have to believe me. I couldn't be the reason you four lost everything you've worked for."

Again, I bury my face in her neck. I can't speak through the emotion clogging my throat. This entire time, she did this for me. She let him get away with putting his hands on her, these marks on her, because she was protecting me.

She fucking owns me.

"Never," I mumble the words. "You will never lose me," I assure her. "I need you to tell me you understand what I'm telling you. I need to know that you understand that I'm not me without you."

"I love you," she cries.

Not gonna lie, I can feel the burn behind my eyes. Yep, he's a dead man. I stand and set her on the couch, looking over at Tristan and Gavin. "I need one of you to stay here with her, and one of you to help me hide the fucking body."

"Cole! No." Stacy stands and grabs my arm. "You can't! I need you here."

"Stacy, babe, he has to pay for what he did to you." Stepping back, I gently push both of her sleeves up her arms. "Look," I croak out. "Look at his mark on you. I can't let him get away with that."

"Cole," Kacen warns.

"You stay with your wife." I turn to Tristan and Gavin. "Which one of you is staying and which one of you is digging?"

"C-man, there's another way," Tristan says.

"The fuck there is!" I roar. "Do you see this? Do you see what he did to her? I can't fucking breathe knowing he's getting off scot-free. I will never let anyone hurt her again. I fucking let him. I took her there. She was there for me and then he put his damn hands all over her. She kept this inside to protect me. I fucking failed her, but I won't do it again."

I head toward the door, but Stacy runs to jump in front of me. Tristan and Gavin move back in the already tight space of the tour bus.

"Please," she begs.

"Stace, I need you to move." I refuse to put my hands on her to move her. I won't be like him.

She backs up and, just when I think I've won, she leaps into my arms. I have no choice but to catch her, placing my hands on her ass, holding her up. She wraps her arms and legs around me.

"Please, hear them out. There has to be another way. You go to him and he presses charges, I lose you. They lose you. Everything you've worked for is washed down the drain. Please," she reasons.

With the grip she has on me, I no longer fear that she will fall. I remove my hands from her ass and bind them around her, crushing her against me. "He hurt you," I say against her neck. "I'm so fucking sorry." My voice breaks.

"Just hear them out. For me?"

I will never deny this girl anything. "I don't like it."

"He's gone, man." Gavin holds up his phone. "I just texted Cassidy. He's on a fight back to Nashville as we speak."

At his words, I deflate. I can't hop on a plane and leave her, not with her begging me to stay.

"Hear me out. If you still want to go after him, then that's what we'll do. I'll be your wing man, or should I say shovel man," Tristan jokes.

Even though the moment is far from funny, I can't help but chuckle at him.

"Okay," I finally concede. That doesn't mean I'm letting him get away with this, though. It only means he gets to live a day or two until I can get to him.

He fucked with the wrong girl.

CHAPTER 38

I WANT TO CRY WITH relief. Hell, who am I kidding—I want to cry regardless. The last twenty-four hours have been hell. But I'm worried about Cole. I've never seen him this angry before.

"Let's sit." His lips are against my ear.

I don't let go of him for fear that he will change his mind and race off the bus to the nearest airport.

He settles on the couch, me sitting sideways in his lap. Our arms are locked around each other, neither willing to let go.

"Give it to me," he says gruffly.

"First, Stacy, babe, are you willing to press charges against this asshole?" Gavin asks.

I stiffen. I chance a look at Cole and his eyes are locked on me. He gives me a hard nod. No argument there.

"Yes," I confirm.

"We need to call the police and file a report. They need to take pictures." He points to my arms.

I watch as he puts his phone to his ear and alerts the bands security team to call the cops.

"Okay, what else?" I ask.

"He's going to want to cut a deal. He's going to try and get us to drop the charges."

"Fuck that!" Cole barks.

"Calm down. I didn't say we would. Our contract with the label is up in, what, four months? I say we get him to release us. We hate the way he runs things. This is finally our chance to open our own label. We bring Bobby and Cassidy with us."

"How does this make him suffer?" Tristan asks.

"I've been spending a lot of time at the label. I hear things. The staff is all too willing to spill what they know. The label is going under. He can't manage it for shit. He blows through money, drinking and rumored drugs, although I have no proof."

"Again, how does that hurt him?"

"We make him think she's willing to drop the charges, if he releases us. He's not the sharpest tool in the shed. He inherited the label from his grandfather. He'll fall for it. He releases us from our contract and Stacy continues with pressing charges. We're in the press constantly. You and Stacy need to be open about this, give interviews even and get the public, our fans, on our side. Hell, after the show tonight, they already love you two."

"So, we trick him?" I ask.

"Yes. He'll go away for a few years at least, from the looks of those bruises, and the . . . inappropriate touching."

Cole growls.

"Then what?" I'm trying to see how this protects them. "You're losing your label. How is that good for the band?"

"Well, we'll no longer be clients of Stone Records. I'm in tight with the board members, and I know they'll have to sell," Gavin says, like I should understand where this is going. My brain is too jumbled to make sense of it.

"We swoop in and buy the label." Kacen is grinning.

"Fucking brilliant!" Tristan bellows.

"Babe?" I address Cole.

His head snaps toward mine. I watch as his lips lift in a slow, sexy smile. "I like it," he says, leaning in and kissing me. "Say it again?"

Say what again? I must be wearing a confused look because he places his lips next to my ear.

"You called me 'babe.'" Pulling back, he cups my cheek. "I want to hear it again." His eyes are pleading, as though maybe he didn't hear me right.

"Babe." I keep my voice low, just for him.

His lips cover mine, slow and easy.

Give and take.

Pulling back once again, he rests his forehead against mine. "I'm so fucking sorry, baby. He'll never touch you again. I swear to you."

"I'm okay. It's just a few bruises. I was worried about you. I didn't want you to lose what you've worked so hard for over me. In my mind, that led to me losing you, and that just isn't an option for me," I tell him.

"Not gonna happen." He looks over at Gavin. "What do we need to do?"

Gavin looks at me. "You ready for this, Stacy?"

Cole squeezes my leg.

"As I'll ever be. Are you all sure about this? I don't want to ruin anything for you."

Gavin nods as he pulls out his phone I'm assuming to alert our security team to bring the cops to the bus.

"What you need to understand is that you are one of us." Kacen points at Cole. "He loves you, we love you—it's that simple. We're going to push through this, and it might actually work to our advantage. An established label is a hell of a lot easier to get off the ground. Not to mention it's in Nashville, close to home."

"We've talked about this as a group for a while now, more so since Kace got married. This has always been the plan as we all start to settle down," Cole says.

"Let's do it."

Gavin unlocks the door. "Bring them in, guys."

I move to sit beside Cole instead of on his lap. Gavin mentioned pictures. Cole keeps his arm around my waist as I sit on the edge of the couch. A female officer steps onto the bus.

"Ma'am, I'm Detective Morris. Is there a private place where we can talk?" She looks around at the guys. They can be a little intimidating.

"Here's fine. They're family."

Cole gives my hip a gentle squeeze; I assume that means he approves. I start my story from the beginning, telling her about the run-in outside the bus and every detail of last night. Cole never stops touching me; rubbing circles on my back, kneading my shoulders, squeezing my hip among other things, his hands stay on me. He handles hearing the story again better than I thought he would. His grip would tighten, and I'm pretty sure I heard him growl a few times, but other than that, he kept his cool.

"I'm going to need to take some pictures." Detective Morris pulls a Polaroid camera from her bag.

Standing, I pull off my long-sleeve Soul Serenade T-shirt. Cole gasps and I laugh. "I have on a cami," I tell him.

"Woman," he says, shaking his head.

I'm filled with relief at our banter. It gives me hope that this is not going to turn out like I had originally thought. The guys seem like they're okay with the plan, and Cole . . . well, he still wants me. I just hope Gavin knows what he's talking about, that this will all turn out good for them. The Soul Serenade guys are my biggest concern at this point.

"Thank you. I'll get this processed and there will be a warrant out for his arrest." Detective Morris looks at Cole. "You make sure she's not alone until we catch him."

"I've got her," he says, pulling me close.

Once Detective Morris is gone, I turn to Cole. "Are you sure this is the best way? What if this doesn't work like you think it will?"

"It's going to be fine. Besides, it doesn't matter. We have two weeks left of this tour and then our contract ends a few months after that. Regardless, once this tour is done, so am I. I will not continue to work for Stone Records with Wilson at the helm."

"This was our long-term backup, if you will. I want to spend more time with Logan and the baby. I don't want to miss a minute. This is something we've talked about. Don't stress," Kacen adds.

"If it weren't for the fans, I would say fuck the rest of the tour," Tristan chimes in.

"No shit. I would hate to disappoint them, but it pisses me off that that fucker is going to make money off us," Gavin remarks.

"You can't." I cover my face with my hands. "Your fans will hate me."

"Pretty sure your boy took care of that. Our fans are loyal, and he told them he loves you tonight. When this gets out, they're going to rally around you. That's only going to help us, and you," Kacen explains.

"Sorry to interrupt," Bruce the driver says. "We need to get on the road if we're going to make our next destination."

"Let's do it," Kacen responds.

"Babe, let's go to bed. It's been a long-ass night, and I need to hold you." Cole stands and holds his hand out for me.

"Wait!" Logan reaches out and pulls me into a hug. "Don't you ever keep something like this from me again. Ever. Do you understand?" she scolds me.

"Yeah, I just—"

"No excuses. Stacy, it could have been so much worse." Her voice cracks.

"It could have, but it wasn't. It's just a few bruises that will be gone in a few days," I try to soothe her. "Get some rest. We can talk more tomorrow." I hate putting this extra stress on her and the baby.

Lacing my fingers through Cole's, I allow him to lead me to our bunk. Once we're settled, my back to his front and his arms around me, I take what feels like my first breath since last night.

"I want to kill him."

"I know you do, but you can't. I need you."

"You should have told me last night."

"Cole. . . ."

"No, I know why you didn't. I get it, I do." He pauses before saying, "I need to see you."

I roll over, which is not the easiest feat in our cramped space. When we finally get settled, he cups my cheek. The rough pad of this thumb traces across my lips.

"I need to know that you understand what this is. I love you, Stacy. It's not a crush, not a fling, not just sex. This is more, more than anything has ever been or ever will be. You and me, that's what's important. Nothing, not even my career, can touch this, touch us."

The tears have already started to fall; I've lost count of my breakdowns today. His thumb moves from my lips to wipe underneath my eye.

"You come first. I need to know that the next time you need me you will remember this moment right here. No matter what it is, you come first. Always."

"I love you," I sob.

Cole tucks me into his chest and I let the tears fall. I cry for the man who is holding me like I'm a precious gift, for his bandmates, for Logan. I cry just to wash away the drama and the emotions of the last twenty-four hours.

With his words, Cole Hampton just made it impossible for me to ever love anyone else. Never. Not the way that I love him. He's it for me, and that feels amazing.

CHAPTER 39

COLE

THESE LAST TWO WEEKS HAVE been bittersweet. The crowds have been on point, but none of us are really into it. Wilson was arrested, but of course that fucker made bail. It makes me sick to think that Soul Serenade fans thought we made that happen. That is unfortunately the nature of the beast.

My girl, though, she's doing great. Her bruises are almost gone except for a few small spots. That's a relief, considering every time I look at her, at them, it's a constant reminder of what he did to her. I don't know what I would have done if it had been worse. More than likely I would have been behind bars with no parole.

After tonight's show, we're wheels up until we reach Nashville. It's going to be good to be home, in my bed. That is as long as Stacy is there with me. I've gotten used to sleeping with her tucked in close, and I don't think I could sleep now without her. She knows I'm committed to her, to us. Beyond that, we've not really talked about it.

That doesn't mean I haven't thought about it, though. I do, every fucking day. I worry about how things will be when we get home. I see her every day, I hold her every night.

I don't want that to change.

"Hey, man, you look deep in thought," Kacen says, dropping into the chair beside me.

We're waiting for our final sound check of the tour. Tonight, we have two local bands opening for us. We're just waiting for them to finish up.

"Yeah, got a lot on my mind."

"Wilson?"

"Mostly. The meeting is in two days. Gav says he's got it handled. He says that I can't be there, but I need to be, Kacen. I need to look that Cock Sucker in the eye when I knock him the fuck out for touching her. I want to kill him," I seethe.

"I think it's best if Gavin and I go. We've talked about it. We know what to say. We have a plan. You just hang with the girls while we put the wheels in motion."

"How do I do that? How do I not defend her? Everything in me tells me that I need to lay his ass out."

"She needs you, Cole. That's more important. Trust us to take care of this, to ensure that he gets what's coming to him."

"Fuck," I run my fingers through my hair.

"Focus on your girl. She's what's important. We got your back. You can't hold her in jail," he warns me.

He's right. Stacy is all that matters. "That's the other thing," I confess.

"I figured."

"I need the number to the relator you used when you bought your house."

"Buying, are you?"

I nod. "I want to. It's time to sell the condo and buy a home. One I hope Stacy will be living in with me."

"It's something else, isn't it?" he asks.

"What do you mean?"

"Getting serious. When you're single, you look at all the guys who are tied down and wonder what the hell they were thinking. Why pass up new ass every night?" He finishes off his bottle of water in one long gulp. "Then you meet her. The one person you can't seem to spend enough time with. The one you can't seem to hold long enough, kiss long enough. That one person makes all those other guys look like fools."

"Pretty much," I confirm.

"Good talk." Kacen laughs as he taps me on the shoulder and walks off.

"Hey!" I yell after him. "I need that number."

"Check your phone." He smirks and keeps walking.

Digging my phone out of my pocket, sure enough, he texted me the information for the realtor. I quickly save the contact, type a message, and hit Send. No point in putting this off. I know what I want.

I set up a conference call tomorrow to go over the contract details and gave the realtor some specs for what kind of house I'm looking for. With a little more pep in my step, I make my way backstage. Sound check should be starting soon. Just a few more hours and this tour is over. Our time with Stone Records and our connection with that fucker Wilson will be finished.

Time for new beginnings.

This show, like all the others on this tour, is electric. The crowd is wild, and we as a band are feeding off their energy. As we get ready to sing the last song, Kacen hesitates, and I know it's because we don't know what's next. Everything is changing. We're starting our own label, so who knows if we'll tour again.

This could be it.

Glancing over at Stacy, I know I have no regrets with that decision. And I know Kacen feels the same. It's Gavin and Tristan I worry about. Although, the duo seem to be taking this all in stride. I think it helps that as a band, we've talked about this forever, almost since the day we were signed. We didn't want to be washed-up rock stars—we wanted more out of life. Kace more so than the rest of us. He used to tell us that we would come to his way of thinking. If it were any other man, they would have already been saying "I told you so." Not Kacen. He's just that guy. The one who has a good head on his shoulders, the protector.

He gets it.

"This is an emotional night for us," Kacen says into the microphone. "You see, there are some big life changes coming our way. I, for one, am about to be a father." The crowd roars their approval. "Life is a roller coaster, and we've enjoyed every fucking minute!"

Gavin, Tristan and I speak our agreement into our mics.

"This is the last night of the 'Make Love' tour." The crowd goes crazy. "How many of you out there plan on making love tonight?"

The response is deafening.

"Let me get some love for my man, Tristan, on the drums." He holds his mic out to the crowd. "How about a little for my man, Gavin, on bass?" Again, he holds the mic out to them, and they don't hesitate to show their love. "And over here." He points to me. "We have my man, Cole, on lead guitar." Kacen holds his hand out to the crowd again. "And, of course, I saved the best for last." He smirks as he points to himself. "What do you say, Michigan? Do we want to bring this fucking house down?"

Earsplitting, thunderous screams erupt. "We are Soul Serenade!" Gavin's deep voice booms through the arena.

Tristan taps off the beat to our very first single, "Even Matter," and you can barely hear it over the crowd. The feeling that gives me is a rush like no other. To know they're cheering for us and our passion, for the music. It's an awe-inspiring experience. The only thing that has ever come close to that for me is being inside Stacy. Watching her fall apart at my touch.

"Does it even matter," Kacen starts to sing, and I let myself get lost in the moment, my hands sliding over the strings. I just play.

Three minutes and forty-six seconds later, it's over. The Soul Serenade "Make Love" tour is complete. It's been a wild ride for sure.

Instead of rushing off to the girls, we all just stand in our places in the dark, listening to the crowd yell our names.

Bittersweet.

We all must be thinking the same thing because before I know it, we've all gathered around Kacen.

"One hell of a show," Tristan states.

"Fucking nailed it," Gavin adds.

"The crowd was on fire," I say.

'We'll be back." Kacen's comment has our attention. "I don't know in what capacity, but it's in our blood. We're going to give other bands this same opportunity to see what it's like to be up here in the lights with thousands screaming their name. However, we'll be back. Even if it's just an award show, or a local charity event. We will be back. I want my son to see this. I want him to strive to reach for his dreams."

"I hear ya, man," Gavin agrees.

"Holy shit! You guys kicked ass." Logan rushes into Kacen's arms. Well, as fast as her eight-months-pregnant body allows her.

Stacy wraps her arms around my waist from behind. I'm sweaty as hell, but my girl doesn't seem to mind. She locks her hands around my waist and I cover them with my own.

"I can't believe I'm about to say this shit," Tristan speaks up, "but my ass is beat. I am so ready to be at home in my bed. Let's do this." He motions to the exit sign at the back of the stage.

He gets no argument. I turn to face Stacy and give her a quick kiss, pulling away before I lose myself in her. Tristan leads the way as we leave the "Make Love" tour behind us.

CHAPTER 40

Stacy

"HOME SWEET HOME," TRISTAN MUMBLES as the bus rolls past the Welcome to Nashville sign. We drove through the night, but it's hard to sleep when the bus is bouncing down a construction zone. For me, it's more than that. Cole and I haven't discussed how things will be now that the tour is over. He's finally convinced me that he's in this, but all we've ever known in our relationship is the tour bus. I'm nervous and don't know what to expect now that we're home. On the bus, there was no space; he may want that now that we're back. I've gotten used to his arms around me at night and waking up to him each day. I don't want that to change, but I don't want to turn into a stage-five clinger. I do not want to be that girl.

It's only been three months. Sure, I've known him longer and he chased me longer, but still . . . only three months of really knowing him.

"Hey." Cole pulls me onto his lap from where I'm sitting beside him on the couch. "You coming home with me?"

Can he read my mind? "Is that what you want?"

"Yes."

No hesitation. "I'll need to go visit my parents."

"We can do that. Later today?" he asks.

"No, not today. Can we go tomorrow? I really just want a nice, long, hot shower and to lounge on a big bed or full-size couch. Anything that is not on this bus."

He chuckles, hiding his face in my neck. "Done."

Just like that.

When the bus pulls into Kacen's drive, there are already three cabs waiting. Cole told me to grab my essentials and we would get the rest later. The driver will park the bus out back; apparently, he has a car here. This business is so different, and there is still a lot to learn.

The cab ride to Cole's condo is short. As he unlocks the door, I have butterflies in my stomach. This is not a hotel room, or the bus. This is his space.

This is real.

Opening the door, he holds it, ushering me in before him. "Make yourself at home. I'm just going to throw our bags in my room."

He strides off toward the hallway while I take in my surroundings. Dark leather couch, big-screen television—and when I say big, I mean takes-up-one-wall big. There are a few awards and pictures of his family. If it weren't for those few pictures, this would be the normal bachelor pad—the clean version, of course.

"No food since we've been gone for so long. You want takeout? I can order groceries online so we don't have to go out."

"I've heard about that new service in some areas, but I've never used it."

"Yeah, it's nice for the most part. I'm not a big fan of people knowing where I live, but the place prides itself on confidentiality. Or so they say." He grins. "So far, no issues. So, what will it be?"

"I'm good with whatever." I smile.

"Hey, now." He walks to where I'm standing and wraps me in his arms. "Where's my girl? You've never had a problem telling me what you want before. What's wrong?"

I return his hug and sigh against his chest. "I don't know. Nothing, really. I just don't know. . . . We're no longer on tour."

He stiffens. "What the fuck does that matter?"

"I don't know if it does."

"Sweets, you're going to have to break it down for me."

I can tell that I've upset him, and that's not what I want. I need to get out of my own head. He wants me here. "It's just . . . I don't want to be in your way. On the bus, you didn't have an option—there was no getting a break from me. Now that we're home, you can." I shrug. Once the words leave my mouth, I know how idiotic they sound, but it's been an emotional few weeks and he's right—I need to tell him what I'm thinking.

"Come here." Lacing his fingers through mine, he guides us to the couch. He sits and pulls me onto his lap. "You want to know what I want?" he asks.

I give a slight nod, while those chocolate-brown eyes of his bore into me.

"I want you. All the time. I want your life so goddamn intertwined with mine that I don't know the difference between you and me. I want it to be us. So to answer your question, no, I most certainly do not want space from you. My goal is to eliminate that space as much as possible."

Then he kisses me.

Slowly at first, but then his soft yet firm lips demand a response. I immediately open for him, allowing his tongue to push past my lips. Cole's hand rests on my thigh; he begins to caress it, and the simple act sends currents of desire through me.

He lifts me in his arms and we're moving. I assume we're headed to his bedroom. It's the touch of the soft mattress against the back of my thighs that confirms my suspicion.

"Beautiful," he says as I slide back on the bed. "Do you have any idea how long I've imagined you here?"

I shake my head. I have no idea, but if the look in his eyes tells me anything, it's been a while.

"I need you naked, sweets."

Losing all inhibitions, I reach for the hem of my shirt and pull it over my head. I toss it on the floor and look up at him from under my lashes. My silent taunt telling him it's his turn.

He doesn't take the hint; he just stares at me as if he can't believe I'm actually here. That alone sends my desire for him into overdrive. Climbing to my knees, I move to the edge of the bed. His hand cups the back of my head as he moves in for another kiss. This one is frantic and messy and perfect. It matches my craving for him.

"This needs to go," I say between kisses, pulling his shirt up his toned abs.

With a groan, he releases my lips to pull his shirt over his head. He doesn't stop there, making quick work of ridding himself of all clothing separating his skin from mine.

"You're overdressed." He smirks.

"What are you going to do about that?"

His deep chuckle fills the room and a smile lights up his face. "Come here, you." He reaches for my shorts and has them unbuttoned and sliding over my hips along with my panties in a matter of seconds. "Lie back."

I do as he says and lift my hips, allowing him easier access to finish undressing me. I manage to move myself back on the bed and he stalks after me. His body is now hovering over mine. He leans in for a kiss and I drink him in.

Breaking the kiss, he reaches over and fumbles around in the drawer of the nightstand. I watch as he pulls out a condom. I reach for it, but he holds his hand out of reach.

"You can't, sweets. I want this to be slow. I need to make love to you, but if I let you do this,"—he holds up the condom—"it will be over before it starts."

Good to know he's just as affected as I am. I watch unashamed as he rolls the condom over his length and settles back on top of me. He keeps his weight on his forearms, careful not to crush me.

His hands are in my hair, smoothing it back, his eyes intense as he watches me. A soft, quick kiss to my lips and he's pushing inside. "I love you, Stacy," he says against my lips.

I don't reply. I can't. All I want is for him to move, to take care of this ache that he caused. I bury my nails into his back and pull him toward me, lifting my hips.

"Slow," he whispers.

"Cole." My voice rests somewhere between begging and moaning.

He bites down on his bottom lip as his hips slowly rotate against mine. "Slow." He groans it this time.

I can tell that it's taking all his restraint not to let loose. I lift my hips again, moving my hands to his lower back and pulling him into me.

"Fuck," he moans, burying his face in my neck.

"Yes, that's the point," I urge him.

"I want to savor you. I've wanted you in my bed for so long and now that you're here—"

I interrupt him. "Now that I'm here, you're going to fuck me. I want you, all of you. Don't hold back, please," I beg.

I see the moment that he relents; his eyes grow darker and a wicked grin graces his lips. "Hold on, sweets," he warns, and then unleashes at my request.

Holding on is all I'm capable of as he takes control, giving me exactly what I've asked for.

I meet him stroke for stroke, every thrust growing closer to the edge.

"You there, sweets?" he asks. His voice alone tells me he's losing control.

"Yes!" I cry as we both fall into the blissful existence that is just us. Cole and Stacy.

Nothing else matters.

CHAPTER 41

TODAY IS THE DAY GAVIN and Kacen are meeting with Wilson. He thinks they're going to talk to him about taking a deal, and they are, kind of. The plan is to get him to release us from our contract with the thought that Stacy will drop the charges. What he won't know is that, unless we have an attorney there—which we won't—it means nothing.

Our attorney already drew up the paperwork for terminating our contract early. Gavin has spoken to the board members and they're all appalled at what Wilson did to Stacy. He claims they're behind us.

I begged them to let me go, since I still have some payback to give him for hurting her, but Stacy shot it down before my boys could even open their mouths. Turns out, my girl is fiercely protective like me. I have to admit that, as I lie here holding her in my arms watching the sunrise, I think I got the better deal. Gavin and Kacen have to be at the label in thirty minutes.

I look down at my sleeping beauty and the last twenty-four hours replay in my mind. Once I had her in my bed, I wanted her everywhere. I want to be able to walk into my condo and see her. I want to be flooded with memories of our time together. Surely that will hold me over during the times she's not with me, right?

Then again, once this place sells, the effort will have been lost, but not forgotten. I could never forget a single second of my time with her. We'll just have to christen the new house, the one I hope to buy soon. The realtor sent me an e-mail; there is a house just down the street from Kace and Logan that just came up for sale. There isn't even a sign in the yard yet. I know the place, and I'm crossing my fingers that she falls in love with it. I know she'll love the idea of living so close to her best friend. Yes, I want her to move in. I want it all with her. Every fucking cliché you can think of, I want it.

We're supposed to see the house at ten this morning; I didn't want to take the chance of someone buying it out from under me. Not to mention that I don't want to wait to put my plans in motion. I want to build a life with her. It will also help both of us keep our minds off what's going on with the label and Wilson. I trust Gavin, so I have to have faith that it's all going to work out.

Regardless, I have her. She's all that matters.

"Hey," she says in her sleepy, sexy-as-hell voice.

"Morning, sweets." I kiss her temple.

"How long have you been up?" She stretches and I'm transfixed by her naked body on display before me.

"Cole." She giggles.

I fucking love that sound.

"A while. We have somewhere to be at ten."

She sits up. "What time is it? Where are we going?

"It's just after seven. My realtor sent me an e-mail, and there is a house I want to go look at."

"Really? What's wrong with this place?" she asks, confused.

It hits me that I've yet to fill her in on any of my plans. "I think it's time for a house." I shrug as if it's not a big fucking deal, but it *is* a big fucking deal. I just can't let her know that yet. I have a few other surprises up my sleeve. "Things are changing. We're going to be in town for longer periods of time. This was never a permanent solution."

She studies me like she knows I'm not telling her the whole story. "I guess I better get dressed."

She's out of bed and across the room before I can stop her. I don't protest, just watch her firm ass until it disappears behind the bathroom door. I want to join her, but then I'll want to ravish her and we don't have time for that. Besides, she needs a break after yesterday.

I grab some clothes and go to the guest bathroom to shower, alone. Time to put plans for the future in motion.

"This is it? This is the house?" Stacy asks with excitement in her voice.

"Yeah." I smile at her.

"Logan and Kacen are right down the street. How awesome is that?" she squeals. "I mean, that would be convenient, right? For the band and the label and all that?"

She tries to downplay her excitement, but her little outburst tells me that my next phase is going to be easy. I thought I would have to pull out some persuasion tactics, but after her reaction, I don't think it will be necessary. It's as though she added herself into the equation of living next door to her best friend and then thought better of it.

"Let's take a look," I say, pulling the keys from the ignition.

Stacy is out of the car and bouncing on her heels waiting for me. Lacing my fingers through hers, we make our way to the front door. It pulls open just as I'm about to knock and the realtor, Tom something or other, is there to greet us.

"Mr. Hampton, good morning. It's nice to officially meet you," he says, all business.

I shake his hand. "You too. This is my girlfriend, Stacy." She also reaches out and shakes his hand.

"Well, let's get started. I like to give my clients a run-down of the property and leave you free to roam without me hovering over your shoulder. It's six bedrooms, eight baths, four-car attached garage, state-of-the-art kitchen," he rambles on the specs of the house. "I'll be in the kitchen if you need me, take your time," he finally says.

I motion for Stacy to go ahead of me. I want to see this place through her eyes, want to make sure she'll be happy here. I know I will be if she's here with me.

I follow behind her as she goes from room to room, pointing out all the features she loves. Nothing so far that she hates. The master bedroom has a huge walk-in shower with a million showerheads, which was on my list of must-haves. I could very easily remodel, but it will be nice to not have to. I'm pretty sure my girl loves this place.

"Cole, this kitchen is gorgeous," Stacy says in awe.

She's right. It's state of the art, dark cabinets with granite countertops and all stainless steel appliances. Her eyes sparkle as she takes it in. I can see her making dinner, or maybe baking with our kids. Yeah, I went there, and I'm fucking stoked at the thought.

"Let's take a look outside," I suggest.

She leads the way out to the back deck. The view is amazing—in-ground pool, hot tube fire pit, you name it. "Wow," she breathes.

I wrap my arms around her and pull her against my chest as we take in the backyard. "So, what do you think?"

"I think it's amazing. You?"

Yes, you are. "You think you could see yourself living here?"

She's quiet.

No response.

"Stacy?"

She turns in my arms and her eyes shimmer with tears she's holding back. "You asking me to move in with you?"

"I thought it was a given. Where I go, you go," I respond.

A lone tears falls from her eye. "Really?" She smiles.

I want to put that smile on her face every fucking day.

"I want you with me. Always," I say, leaning down to rest my forehead against hers. "What do you say, sweets? Will you move in with me?"

I hear the door open as Tom steps out onto the deck. 'What do you think?" he calls out to us.

"Stace?" I leave the ball in her court.

Pulling back, she looks up at me from under her lashes. "Yes."

Relief washes through me. Step one complete. Looking over my shoulder, I address Tom, "We'll take it."

"Perfect." He claps his hands together. "It's immediate occupancy, so all we have to do is sign the paperwork and it's all yours."

"You just bought a house," she beams.

"No, baby, *we* bought a house. This is your home now. Your home with me." I kiss her slowly, tasting her, relishing the moment. Our first official step toward the future.

The ringing of my cell phone pulls me away from her. It's the call I've been trying not to think about.

Gavin.

"Hey, man," I greet him.

"C, you around?" he asks.

"Yeah, what's up?" I'm playing it cool, but I'm nervous as fuck.

"We're at Kacen's. Tristan is on his way, thought we could have a little get-together and go over the meeting." He says it as if we'll be discussing the weather.

"Be right there." I end the call. "Gavin wants us all to meet at Kacen's. They're back," I tell Stacy.

She nods, the smile on her face vanishing as worry sets him. I tell Tom to get everything in order and to call me when it's ready, then head down the road, not even a mile to Kacen's. I want to be excited that we'll be living so close, but first I need to know what the outcome of today was.

Tristan pulls in behind us. The three of us are quiet as we enter the house, following voices to the living room. Kace and Logan are on the small loveseat, their hands clasped around her growing belly. Gavin sits in the chair, Tristan taking the other while I lead Stacy to the couch. I pull her onto my lap, needing her close for this conversation. She grounds me.

"Well," Tristan asks.

Gavin smirks. "He signed them. We're free from our contract with Stone Records. He agreed to all our terms."

I take what feels like my first breath in weeks.

"He was wasted, higher than a kite. We also got his recorded confession from that night. You won't have to testify," Kacen tells Stacy.

"Wh-what? How?" she stammers.

I rub circles on her back, though I'm not sure if it's to soothe her or me.

Logan smiles, tears in her eyes at the news.

"I called Detective Morris, wanted to keep her in the loop with what was going on. They wired us." Gavin points to his chest. "It's official, so it will hold up in court. He even went a little further and divulged what his plans were had he not been interrupted."

I clench my fists.

"That's why I didn't want you there, man. Even without that, you wouldn't have been able to hold your temper. Having Tristan stay back was a decoy of sorts. Couldn't have you thinking you were the only one." Kacen smirks.

Stacy hops off my lap and rushes to Kacen. Leaning down, she hugs him then she and Logan share a crying hug as well. She stands and heads toward Gavin, who rises to greet her as she hugs him tight. For good measure, my girl also leans down and gives my man Tristan some love as well. Then she comes right back to me, where she belongs.

"I don't know how to thank you," she cries into her hands.

"You're family, Stacy. Remember that," Gavin explains.

"Good news all around today," I remark.

"What did I miss?" Tristan asks.

The others are looking at me with the same question in their eyes. "We"—I give her leg a gentle squeeze—"bought a house."

"No shit. Congratulations!" Tristan says.

"That's big-time, C," Gavin adds. "Where is this casa al la Hampton?"

I look at Kacen. "Right down the street the house with the brick entrance gates."

"I love that house," Logan chimes in.

Kacen nods; this isn't news to him. "Congrats, man."

The guys and I start talking about the next phase. The board is holding a meeting Monday morning and the decision will be made to sell the label. Gavin has already turned in our offer in writing. We discuss options and how we want to process, even the name—we refuse to leave it as Stone Records. Stacy and Logan are laughing and smiling in their own conversation.

Can it ever get any better than this?

CHAPTER 42

IT'S HARD TO BELIEVE THAT we've lived in this house a month today. Between Wilson's sentencing, buying all the furniture we need to fill this place, and the guys buying out Stone Records, this month has been hectic. Not to mention that baby Warren arrived two weeks ago. He's so precious. Andrew Michael Warren stole my heart the minute I met him. They decided on Andrew, with Andrews being Logan's maiden name. It's fitting with all the name play those two have done in their relationship.

I've spent a lot of time over there, watching him while they nap. It's not exactly a hardship to hold that little guy. Logan says I spoil him, but that's my job as Aunt Stacy.

Today, we're having a house warming of sorts. We're finally settled not only in the house, but in our lives. Wilson is behind bars. Turns out, his confession wasn't just about what he did to me or planned to do; he also confessed to laundering money and a slew of other criminal offenses. He won't be seeing freedom for years to come.

The guys finally decided on a name—Soul Records. They wanted to incorporate who they are into this label. Having put their heart and souls into music, I thought it was fitting. Logan and I both tried to convince them to just call it Soul Serenade, but they shot it down. The compromise was Soul Records, and I have to admit I'm digging it.

"Your dad just called, they're on the way," Cole says as he comes in from lighting the grill.

"Why didn't he call me?"

He smirks.

Dad and Cole hit it off immediately; apparently, they now have a budding bro-mance. I act like it's weird, but in all honesty it's comforting to know they get along so well. They are the two most important men in my life. Mom loves him too; he pulled out all the Hampton charm and she was immediately under his spell. Again, can't blame her.

My phone rings, and I quickly dry my hands from washing the fresh vegetables.

"Hey, Chloe," I say in greeting.

Cole shakes his head. He's not the only one who's formed relationships with family. Chloe and I hit it off right away, and of course Miss Mia and I are tight as well.

"No, I think we're good. Just make sure you bring your swimsuits," I remind her. "Great, see you soon." I end the call.

Cole startles me when his hands land on my hips. He picks me up and sets me on the counter, and I immediately wrap my legs around him.

"I love you. I love this. These moments." He kisses me softly.

"Hey now, enough of that," Tristan says, joining us.

"Why did you insist on giving them the code?" Cole asks.

I laugh. "They're family." I throw his words from weeks ago back at him.

"Yeah, we're family," Gavin goads him as he leans in and kisses my cheek.

"Hands off my woman." Cole elbows him out of the way.

"Baby, sit down, I got it."

"EEEP!" I jump off the counter and push Cole to the side. He chuckles, knowing exactly where I'm headed. Baby Drew is my weakness. "Aunt Stacy needs her fix," I say, holding my arms out as Kacen pulls Drew from his seat. He immediately hands him over, but not before kissing his little head. Kacen is such a softie for his son.

I settle on the couch beside Logan as we coo over the little man. "You need any help?" Logan asks.

"Nope, we got it under control. You just sit back and relax."

Cole joins us and squeezes in beside me on the couch. "Your husband is checking out my industrial icemaker. He wants one," he tells Logan.

"Yes, he told me about that. I want to see it." She stands. "You okay with him for a minute?"

I look over my shoulder at Cole. "He's big and scary, but I can handle him," I joke.

She laughs. "Good to know, but I meant Drew."

"I got this." I wave her on.

Cole leans in and kisses my neck. "He's pretty cute," he comments.

"Yeah," I say, watching him sleep.

"You want one?" he asks.

Holy shit. "Yeah, I mean, I've always wanted to be a mom. I told you that before this even started." I know I sound defensive, but letting me fall in love with him and then telling me he doesn't want kids is a dick move.

"Hey," he says soothingly. His hands stroke gently up and down my arms. "I wasn't saying I didn't. I was going to suggest throwing away your birth control pills. We've already stopped using condoms," he says matter-of-factly.

I stop breathing.

He wants kids.

With me.

Now.

Am I dreaming?

"Is that what you want?" I manage to ask.

"Yeah," he replies, his voice soft.

"Now, we're not married or even engaged. It hasn't even been a year."

"It was a year ago today that I first laid eyes on you in the club."

"You remember that?"

"I do. Every moment, every word, every kiss, every touch with you is engrained in my memory. I knew the minute I laid eyes on you that you were different. I didn't know at the time that you were going to rock my world."

"You're the rock star," I say stupidly. He's kind of thrown me for a loop here.

He chuckles. "That I am. I'm also the man who is madly in love with you."

"You need one of those," my dad says as he and Mom join us in the living room.

Oh. My. God.

"That's exactly what I was just telling her," Cole agrees.

I elbow him, which causes him to laugh. He kisses my shoulder then stands to shake Dad's hand. They leave to find the other guys. Mom is still laughing at what I can only assume is my horrified expression at my father and Cole discussing me being pregnant.

"Drew, what are we going to do with these crazies?" I ask the sleeping baby.

"Unca Cowe!" Mia screams as she walks through the door.

"In the kitchen," Cole yells.

I hear the pitter-patter of her little feet and she runs toward his voice. "We habing a pwty," she says as she launches herself at Cole. Luckily, he was hunched down and ready for her.

"We are, are you hungry?" Cole asks.

"Yep. What's that?" She points to the potato salad I'm making.

"Aunt Stacy is making potato salad," he tells her.

I stop immediately and just look at him. It's the first time he's ever referred to me as "Aunt" to Mia.

"What?" he asks when he sees me staring at him.

"You called her Aunt Stacy," Chloe happily explains, wearing a huge-ass grin.

Cole shrugs. "Just missing a piece of paper, no point in denying it."

Holy shit. Is this my life? Have I really landed in this fairy tale with this band and this man, the love of my life? My sweet Cole?

"Aunt Stacy, is that stuff good?" Mia asks. She's oblivious to the emotions that are coursing through me.

"Yes, sweetheart, do you want to try it?" I ask, my voice cracking. I need to get it together. This is my life now. I'm not dreaming. I never knew happiness would be this . . . amazing.

Mia shakes her head at a rapid pace, making us all laugh. Grabbing a fork from the drawer, I gather a small bite and offer it to her.

Mia opens her mouth and takes the bite I offer. "Yummy!" She licks her lips. "She yo wife?" she asks Cole.

A smile like no other lights up his face. "She will be, Princess Mia. She will be." He gives me a wink, kisses her on the cheek and then sets her down.

"I go see the baby," she announces and the pitter-patter of her little feet trail off as she enters the living room.

In one long stride, Cole is next to me. His index finger lifts my chin so he can see my eyes. "I love you."

"I love you, too."

"All right, love birds, when can we eat? I'm starving," Tristan asks.

"Here," I laugh at him, "make yourself useful and carry this out to the deck. I'm right behind you. Once Gavin says the meat is done, we are good to go."

Tristan takes the two bowls and heads out the door. "You, G. . . ." His voice trails off as the door closes behind him.

"I'll go gather the rest of the troops." Cole smacks my ass and strolls out of the kitchen.

Dinner was amazing and the house is full of our families. My parents and Cole's are chatting on the deck. Tristan, Gavin and Kyle are talking sports. Logan and Chloe are discussing babies and pregnancies. Chloe is due with baby number two in a couple of months. I'm sitting with Mia as we play with the bubbles I bought for her.

"Aunt Stacy!" she shrieks when I blow a string of bubbles in her direction. She laughs and takes off running.

Cole appears at my side. "Hey, sweets." He kisses my cheek.

I smirk at him as I dip the wand back into the bubbles, catching him off guard when I blow them in his face.

"You little—" I drop the container and take off running. Why, I don't know, since his legs are longer than mine. He catches me easily, swinging me around by my waist. We both fall to the ground in laughter, trying to catch our breath.

"Unca Cowe!" Mia runs into his arms. She's grinning like crazy. "You wuv her?" she asks.

Breathing heavy, wearing a blinding smile, he tells Mia, "Yeah, I love her."

"I know, I was telling you," she replies.

"Oh, yeah, and how do you know?"

"You can't bweave," she says, like we should know where she's going with this.

"I was running," he says, winded.

"No, Unca Cowe. You tode me you get mawied when you can't bweave without her. That's why you running. You needed to bweave. You wuv Aunt Stacy."

Cole hugs her to him. "You're absolutely right, Princess Mia. I can't breathe without her," he says, his eyes locked on mine.

"Yay!" she runs off, chasing a butterfly.

"That's what I told her. That you get married and have babies when you find the one person you can't breathe without. I didn't want to blacken her reception of happily ever after at the time."

I don't say anything, unable to look away from the intensity in his eyes. "Even she can see how much you mean to me. You think ours will be as perceptive?"

Ours.

Our kids.

"Probably," I say, because they will be his. He's the most assured person I've ever met.

"Positive. I'll make sure they see it every day. What it means to need someone to breathe. Hell, all they'll have to do is see me look at you. At least, that's what my mom tells me."

Mia falls into him, wrapping her arms around his neck and giggling. "Piggy back, Unca Cowe." She laughs.

Not one to disappoint, he stands and carries her around the yard.

I watch them play as my heart fills with love.
This is my dream.
This is now my future.

CHAPTER 43

TRISTAN AND GAVIN ARE THE last to leave, staying hours after everyone else. I hate that they're going home to an empty house. Neither of them seems to be in the mood to hook up. There is more going on there, but both are tight-lipped. We spent some time on YouTube listening to some independents waiting to get their big break. Soul Records is searching for that diamond in the rough.

Stacy is upstairs in our room; she's just climbing into bed. "Hey, you can't take that sexy ass of yours to bed without me," I scold her.

"Excuse me, Mr. Hampton, sir." She mock salutes then bursts out laughing.

"Hey," I say, sitting on the bed next to her. "Don't mock me. Besides, my last name is fucking awesome," I tell her. Her green eyes sparkle with happiness, and I know this is it.

"Oh, yeah, and why's that?" she fires back.

I cup her cheek and lean in close, my lips close to hers. My eyes hold her stare. "Because it's going to change yours." I kiss her.

She doesn't kiss me back, so I pull away.

"Wh-what?"

I stand from the bed, bringing her with me. I reach into my pocket and pull out the small blue case that's been there since I got dressed this morning. I chose to wear baggy shorts on purpose. I fall to my knees and look up at her.

"I'll be there to catch you when you fall apart under my touch. I'll be there to catch you when life knocks you down. I'll be there every damn morning when you wake up, and I'll hold you in my arms each night. You're my lover and my best friend." Tears are streaming down her face as I open the box. "Will you also do me the incredible honor of being my wife?" I use her words from all those months ago.

"Cole?" There is question in her voice.

"I love you, Stacy. I can't breathe without you. Mia was right. I was just about to ask you then, but she came back and the moment was lost. I want it all, baby. Marriage, kids, dog—hell, you can even have a white picket fence placed around the property. I want all of it and I want all of you, with my last name, for the rest of our lives."

She drops to her knees, her arms wrapping around my neck. "Yes. YES!" she screams then hugs me tight.

Hell fucking yeah!

Pulling back, I kiss her long and hard. She's mine. I reluctantly break our kiss to slide my ring on her finger. It's a four-carat pear-shaped solitaire.

"Oh, my God, it's beautiful," she gushes, holding her hand out to admire it. "We're getting married," she squeals as she launches herself at me.

I don't waste time getting to the bed; instead, I strip us both down and make love to my fiancée on our bedroom floor.

We're both too exhausted and elated afterward to move to the bed, so I reach up and pull the covers down over us. Luckily, the carpet is plush. Stacy sleeps softly as I adjust her so she's lying against my chest. I'm beat, but sleep won't come. I'm hyped up on life, on her. I never knew I wanted this, but now I couldn't be more certain that this is how it was meant to be. Fate brought her to me, and I will make damn sure that I spend every breath letting her know what she means to me. Not a day will go by that she doesn't feel cherished.

I assure you.

CONTACT
KAYLEE RYAN

Facebook:
www.facebook.com/pages/Kaylee-Ryan-Author

Goodreads:
www.goodreads.com/author/show/7060310.Kaylee_Ryan

Twitter:
@author_k_ryan

Instagram:
Kaylee_ryan_author

Website:
www.kayleeryan.com

ALSO BY
KAYLEE RYAN

With You Series

Anywhere With You

More With You

Everything With You

Stand Alone Titles

Tempting Tatum

Levitate

Just Say When

Unexpected Reality

Soul Serenade Series

Emphatic

Assured

Southern Heart Series

Southern Pleasure

Southern Desire

ACKNOWLEDGEMENTS

My family. Thank you for always supporting me. You will never know how much your support means. I love you.

I love the Indie community. I've met some amazing people during this journey and I am grateful for each and every one of you!!

Sommer Stein, Perfect Pear Creative Covers, your ability to read my mind, and produce a kick ass cover is astounding. I love your face, cover girl! Thank you so much for the amazing cover!

Jamie Walker, thank you for agreeing to be the face of Assured. I wish you much success and best of luck with your future endeavors.

Wander Aguiar; Thank you for doing what you do. The shoot was everything I hoped that it would be.

Tami, Integrity Formatting, you never let me down. You make my words come together in a pretty little package. Thank you so much for making Assured look fabulous on the inside!

Kaylee 2, Jamie, Stacy and Lauren, you ladies have been with me from the very beginning and you will never know how grateful for the friendships that we have formed. You always take time from your families to read anything and everything I throw at you. I love you, ladies! Thank you!

Give Me Books, thank you for hosting and organizing the release of Assured. I appreciate all of your hard work getting this book out there.

To all of the bloggers out there...Thank you so much. Your continued never-ending support of myself, and the entire indie community is greatly appreciated. I know that you don't hear it enough so hear me now. ***I appreciate each and every one of you and the support that you have given me.*** Thank you to all of you! There are way too many of you to list…

To my Kick Ass Crew, you ladies know who you are. I will never be able to tell you how much your support means. You all have truly earned your name. Thank you!

Last but not least, to the readers. You will never know how humbling it is to know that you all are reading my words. I truly love writing and I am honored that I am able to share that with you. Thank you to each and every one of you who continue support me, and my dream of writing.

With Love,

kaylee ryan
AUTHOR

CPSIA information can be obtained
at www.ICGtesting.com
Printed in the USA
LVOW10s0306061217
558821LV00030B/1715/P

9 780986 180088